SKIMMING
STONES

Maria Papas is a Perth-based writer whose fiction, creative non-fiction and academic essays have appeared in various journals including *TEXT*, *Griffith Review*, *Axon* and *The Letters Page*. She holds a PhD from the University of Western Australia, where she is now an Honorary Research Fellow in the School of Humanities. In 2020, the creative component of her PhD won the City of Fremantle Hungerford Award. Currently, she also works as a high school teacher and as a sessional academic. When she is not writing, you can find her by the coast or with family. She grew up in Bunbury, and the landscapes of the south-west often feature in her work.

SKIMMING STONES

MARIA PAPAS

FREMANTLE PRESS

For L & D, with love xx

CONTENTS

CODE BLUE

1

After my sister's illness, the colours of summer became brighter, and the sunsets grew deep. The city we moved to was as glassy and as shiny as my mother had promised. Grass came in much thicker patches than we were ever used to, houses were more uniform than they had been back home by the lake, and rooftops and bitumen roads reflected light in a way that made even black seem white. Our new suburban lives quickly warmed us in the same way sunshine warms sand at the beach, and after a while, even I seemed to forget where we had come from or what we had known. I stopped counting new summers, stopped noticing the passing of seasons. Years passed, and the day at the lake faded not into my memory but perhaps into a deeper part of me. Dad had long left. Harriet and Samuel were gone too. Mum took up study at university, and as for my sister—Emma was something else altogether. Time made me comfortable with forgetting. I looked forward without really knowing that I inevitably also looked back. Perhaps this was why I ended up becoming a nurse, why I stopped believing in karma and magic salts, and why I turned to science and the grounded nature of research instead. Perhaps this was also why I let what happened with Nate happen.

What was it that he said?

'I know you.' And, 'Do you remember me?' and I looked up from my seat at the bus stop where I was waiting to go to work all those months ago, and he looked at me, and he smelt like the sea, as if there was salt in his hair even after washing, and in that moment, I knew that yes, I remembered him.

'I do,' I said. 'Of course, I do.'

'What are you doing here?' I asked. And, 'What have you been up to?'

He told me right from the start that he was married. He didn't hide it. We weren't in a nightclub. He wasn't taking me to bed. There was sweetness to him. I used to know him, and I was once drawn to him, and then suddenly he was there, right there, and my heart was thumping like it had thumped at the lake on the day he first held my hand, and yet we only had minutes, seconds even, before the bus came, and then what?

I asked if he still surfed and if he played the guitar, and he said, yes, he did. He said he was a music tutor now and a father. He was teaching and performing. He had a band, a regular covers-thing down at the local pub on a Friday night, which he did for a bit of fun and to be social, but every now and then he also did a show on his own. He sat on stools in small clubs, and it wasn't big or fancy, and he didn't have lofty dreams of fame, but somehow, he always seemed to fill a room.

At the bus stop, he was light and lightness and all about his child and guitars and what the ocean floor looked like, and I smiled at him and said I was a nurse. In all the time since we last saw one another, I had followed a more conventional path; I had gone to university and become a nurse.

'I can see that,' he said, winking at my uniform.

Then he told me that he was finally studying too now, that fatherhood made him want something more solid. He said he had managed to get into a science degree. 'Genetics,' he said. 'Because, you know.'

And I said, 'I do.'

'I still paint,' I said.

'What do you paint?' he asked.

There was a pause, if you could call it a pause. Then the bus pulled in. Its doors opened. Nate grabbed my hand and pulled me back as I stood to go. 'You happy?'

Another pause.

'Grace?' he said.

'Yes.'

'Come hear me play sometime.'

Sky-high boots; that's what I wore. A black tulle mini. A grey singlet with beads hanging off the straps. I was taller than normal, and far more made-up. I had my hair loosened when usually I wore a ponytail. Smoky eyes. Lipstick even.

Cole, my neighbour from across the road, happened to be arriving home from what seemed like a late-night walk to the deli, and as I unlocked my car door, she stopped by, a tub of ice-cream in hand. She was the first to say it, but not the last: 'Grace, you're beautiful.' She asked, 'Where are you off to?' in that gentle way of hers, and when I told her about the boy I sort-of once knew, about his band and his family, she looked at me, caution written all over her face, and she said, 'Oh Grace, do be careful.'

He was an acoustic storyteller; that's the only way to describe him. He sat on a stool in the spotlight just like he said he would; his tempo was slow, the harmonies did not jump abruptly from one to the next, and his timbre was both soulful and sorrowful. In the breaks between songs he spoke to the crowd as if the crowd was sitting in a lounge room, and when he began again, strumming his guitar to indicate a new song, I clapped. We all did. Somebody wolf-whistled. People cheered. Then the spotlight darkened. I sat at that bar and sipped at my drink. Nate's vocals caught the riffs. His pitch deepened. For a little while, there was nothing other than his voice and his music, but then as the lights above the stage flashed red and blue, I was suddenly reminded of another set of lights—sirens, all the way back from the lake—and it had been such a long time since I had allowed myself to think about those sirens that they caught me by surprise and pulled me not just to that afternoon, but also to the day Nate and I sat in the sprinkling rain while he hummed with his pretend guitar, and the two of us—children that we were—wished not for our imagined futures, but for the lives we led before.

'You haven't changed at all,' he said after the crowd thinned out, and for a long time, almost until the bar closed, we sat together, talked and filled in the blanks of our lives. One type of music flowed easily onto the next—rock and blues and flamenco even—and then he took out his phone and showed me an old clip of himself playing a fat guitar with three pairs of strings. He said he lived in Cuba for the same four years

I studied at university, and maybe it was what he needed to do back then, or maybe it had been a mistake, but instead of a degree, he learned the *tres cubano*, although *tres*, he clarified, was not what I heard that night.

I said, '*Tres cubano* sounds so specific. Why?'

He told me that he was drawn to the movement and the deeper story in the musical score, that it was to do with wanting to know more about his family, his history, and I said, 'I understand,' because I remembered my mother and the way she used to speak of the bouzouki and the dances she learned when she was a child, and I remembered also wishing I knew exactly what those dances were, or which ones belonged to her village, or whether they were the dances of poor people or butchers or those in exile.

Ten minutes passed, fifteen, but not much longer than that, and then right in the middle of all our catch-up chatter, he brushed one hand over mine, and at the same time as I felt the calluses beneath his fingers, I also saw that his wedding ring was full of scratches. 'Nate ...' I said, 'your hands.' He looked towards his thickened skin, and then towards his ring, and because it all seemed to silence him, I said, 'Your wife, is she here?'

He shook his head and said, no, she was home with their boy. These things tired her. It had been three years since she last saw him play.

I said, 'I'm sorry to hear that.'

'It's okay,' he said, 'It's not your fault.' Then he grabbed his phone again and showed me photographs of a fair little toddler with blue and green jelly on his face.

We didn't flirt. We didn't try to turn nothing into something. It was innocuous. He was a married man and he had a child, and I knew all too well what it was to see my parents fall apart. Somewhere in the bottom of a stuffed drawer I had pictures of my family too, which I read differently now that I had grown. It wasn't, for example, an image of my sister dripping ice-cream by her tricycle in as much as it was my father driving off outside the frame of the photograph. I had no intention of being the woman he left my mother for, nor the one who came after. But then I said, 'They don't bother you?'

'What?' he asked.

'Your fingers. The calluses.'

He shook his head and smiled, and then he told me they came from playing so much. He said, 'Do you remember that old Bob Marley tune?'

I didn't know the one he was talking about, so he sang the lyrics of 'Trenchtown Rock' in a funny not-very-good reggae voice, and when he reached the part about music hitting you and you not feeling any pain, he actually screeched his words, and I joked, 'Stick to your normal sound maybe?'

He told me then that it had been like this a long time: since I had known him. Since his brother actually. Since way back then. Music made him forget. If it wasn't for music. This was why he liked to play.

Something passed between us in that moment. I sensed it, and I suspect he did too, but it wasn't yet attraction. More like a bond. 'What do you mean?' I asked, and he confided that there were other things he was ambivalent about. Sadness, for example. Sadness washed over him.

It seemed so incongruent. I thought of the boy I used to know. I remembered him distressed over his brother and over loggers lopping down a tree.

He started it: texting at first, a message here, a message there, just as I was sitting down to dinner, or late, eleven or twelve at night, right at the end of everything. 'Hello,' he would say, and 'How was your day?' Innocent questions that were not so innocent after all. We'd text for hours sometimes—to two or three in the morning. I told myself a whole set of stories: the marriage was bad, or he was leaving it, or in it only for the child. I told myself that this was what people did, that it was just friendship, and that I was the one reading too much into things.

That was how it was in the beginning: as if I wasn't cool or worldly enough. We would share a drink after my shift finished, or lunch, or even a chat at the bar in the breaks of a show. He would phone me unexpectedly. Or else he'd come by with his boy on the back of a pushbike, and it always felt as though the child was so well cared for, so loved, but at the same time there was also something utterly motherless about him, an absence that reminded me of that time back when Emma was sick and I stood in front of my school performances knowing neither of my parents would be in the crowd.

Was I filling the gaps, finding the loopholes that justified what I wanted to do? The boy played on the floor, and while Nate and I shared a simple pot of tea—me with my hands wrapped around the old china cup that I had long ago taken from Harriet, and him drinking out of an ordinary mug—he told me about his first job as a trolley boy and the time he was fired because his best friend's brother stole a packet of cigarettes and blamed him, and then he mentioned his own brother: how this was something David never would have done.

It's hard now to think about how much Nate spoke, how willing he was to share his story, how little he actually said. He smiled whenever he talked about his brother, but it was the same kind of smile I wore when I told him about my family's Easters, cracking painted eggs and eating Red Rooster instead of lamb roast, and so I sat beside him, not yet noticing what these conversations did to my body—the rise in my throat, the bite of my teeth against my lower lip—reacting without knowing.

He said, 'Grace, it all changes when you have kids. Everything you thought you knew, everything you wanted, and then the little shit smiles at you and it's all worthwhile, but it's different. Everything is different.'

I wanted to say, 'Do you love your wife?' and 'Do you still sleep with her? Do you long for her?' but those were not words I allowed out of my mouth.

For a long time, we were *just* friends. That's what we were. But then one thing happened, and then another, and then before I knew it, he was at my door, ringing the bell while slipping his wedding ring into the bottom of the grey satchel he always carried. It would stop me in my tracks, the action of him pulling at his finger and then fumbling with the bag—me on one side of the door, and him on the other, both clear as day and obscured through the frosted glass—and yet I would let him in, the bag rattling with keys and coins and that one piece of gold, and as we made our way through my house, I would simply take the bag, put it in the hallway closet, and pretend it didn't exist.

Nate knew cancer like I knew cancer. We were both from cancer. We shared it like a password between travellers in a foreign country. Or that moment in a crowd when someone says something or another and they carry just the right inflection, an accent you recognise, the sound of home. That's what it was like between him and me. He knew where I had come from. He remembered having first spoken to me, not at the lake like I had thought, but caught in the harsh light of a hospital waiting room all those years ago. In other circumstances, he might have been in my class at school—just as easily the boy who won all the cross-country races as the one who hid cigarettes beneath the railing of the drinks' trough. He could have been anyone with any skill whatsoever—a maths whiz, a budding scientist, a bookworm—but at the lake where I first came to know him and at hospital where he insisted he met me, we were made the same, without distinction. Mine, Nate said, was a hollow face that would scan and forget him just as quickly as I took him in; it was a cloudy face, reminiscent of the face he also once wore.

Nate knew the patterns on the linoleum floor in the hospital as if they were landmarks in his hometown. He memorised the dinner menu, the nurses' names, the medicines which were fed through clear plastic tubes, the channels on the televisions above. We were extras, he and I, but also fixtures. We stood on the other side of closed green doors, in corners of busy rooms and at the edges of small porcelain basins where we diligently scrubbed antibacterial gel onto our palms and over our fingers until the skin on our knuckles began to crack. All the while, we watched our siblings—what they were going through, where they were hurting, and how their throats seemed made of the same tiny rips and tears and broken lines that had appeared on our skin. We poured more of the gel on, kept quiet, and washed and washed and washed, both of us, him with David, and me with Emma, washing our hands, occupying those old halls like the peeling plaster that often fell in flakes to the floor, scrubbing back, scrubbing until it stung. Nate stopped touching the bin, the elevator buttons, toilet doors, toilet seats. We were the siblings, the sidelines, farmed out and left behind, old enough to fend for ourselves, too young to understand.

I was thirteen then, and Emma was four. Nate was my age, but his brother was older, sixteen, and supposedly stronger. We were 'we'. After I found him again, when I was with him, when we lay together in bed, when we whispered and listened to each other speak and not speak, we were 'we'. We understood. We heard. We knew.

And then, when he inevitably returned to his wife, I became 'I' once more. On Friday evening—after everything that happened that day at work, after little Zoe and the sirens, after the seagull at the beach and Nate's wife dressed in draping blue, after all of that—I stood in my front courtyard with my hands wrapped around Harriet's old china cup. Neighbours that had been out had since gone back inside, facades glowed, and streetlights that had long shielded and given me hope, lit the darkness in the same way as they always did, but this time they also dimmed the sky above, making it hard to see the stars. Along Lake Clifton, where I had come from, the Southern Cross, the Pointers and Orion's Belt would have likely been bright pinholes of torchlight behind a worn blanket. Years had passed since my sister fell ill, since my mother left for their long hospital stay and since Harriet took me in. Seasons had cycled. It was November again. The leaves were shadowy on the trees again, and the peppermints and bottlebrushes were in bloom. Pollen was heavy in the air.

2

It had been early on Friday when I arrived at work. The waiting area to our ward was neat and unlit. The fish tank was dark. There were no games on the activity table, no pencils, no pages to colour. The toy kitchen was closed; its doors were shut, and the cups and saucers were neatly packed away. Everything was wiped down, clean, not a speck of paper or food anywhere, yet already the smell of toast wafted through the corridors. It accompanied a shuffling, a crying and the low murmur of parents and nurses and more parents talking. Outside, in the fairy garden on the eastern side of the ward, a little boy laughed and as the sound of his voice carried through an opening door, I remembered being a child in that same garden myself. I remembered Emma, David, Bobby, Mei, Tia, Jake, Arlie, Cameron, and another Grace, a different one, and then, for some reason, it all got to me, the whole sum of it, not because I felt haunted by the children who once occupied these same spaces, but because there were always so many more to come.

That was the thing: the ghosts in our ward were not so much of the past as they were of the future. The patients, whether they were admitted for more than a night or just to Same-Day Care, came and came again. Cohorts of parents knew one another. They met and chatted in the hallways. In the family room, they cooked baked beans and two-minute noodles, the same flavours—salt and popcorn and hot chips—flavours that chemo reorientated the tastebuds towards—recurring over and over. Vegemite and soy sauce for breakfast. Toast and eggs. Tuna sushi.

I used to make those things for Emma too. I used to linger just as the boy in the fairy garden lingered. In the family room, while the kettle whistled, and the television offered a distraction, I would drift off and pretend this was me in boarding school or on camp. I would heat watery Milos and cups of tea. I used to carry this tea to my mum, the hot liquid splashing onto my hands. Those cold corridors and my burning hands. And my mother's face, wrecked and wretched and grateful for something warm to wrap her own hands around. And the paper plates, which I later filled with the crustless toast and soft-boiled eggs that Emma ate for breakfast, lunch and dinner. Me. My jobs. The things that made me useful. But I knew. I knew it wasn't camp. The family room felt like camp, but it wasn't camp.

How can I explain? When you're in it, it is so out of the ordinary you relate it to the closest thing your brain can come up with, the closest *normal* thing, but you know deep in your heart, you know it's not normal at all. The siblings of other patients might feel like distant cousins staying the night, and the older children—if they're in for chemo and not because they have colds or infections that would otherwise isolate them to their rooms—work the coffee or hot chocolate machines like good hosts, but the mood is different. The conversations are strangely out of place. The parents stand in their pyjamas and slippers, holding on to their toiletries. While they wait for their turn at the shower, they talk.

'How did you sleep last night?'

'Not well. I can't handle the beeping.'

'I can't handle the light.'

'We're in Room Seven.'

'We're on high-dose methotrexate. Six trips to the toilet, and then she wet her bed.'

'She's tired. I'm tired. We're grumpy.'

'How's her weight?'

'Not good. Half a kilo from a feeding tube, but she won't eat. Not unless you count salted cucumber and dippy egg.'

'We're on steroids again. Last night I grilled a chicken at two in the morning.'

Those were the conversations that always happened at the coffee machine when the milk was frothing and the steam hissing. Everyone watched the TV, but at the same time they buzzed with their busyness. They tried to comfort one another, tried to talk over the other sounds, the hospital sounds: the beeps, the hums, the hollow tones of newcomers trying to orientate themselves and the polite ways in which those who already understood asked those who didn't yet, 'What happened? Are you new?'

Once, all those years ago, a boy wearing a bathrobe asked me what the problem was with my sister, what was wrong with her.

'Nothing,' I replied. 'There's nothing wrong with her. She's perfect.'

I sat on the couch in front of the television, while yet another family was shown around. I learnt the boy-in-the-robe's name. It was David. He was sixteen, and like my sister, he too had leukaemia.

◉ ◉ ◉

It was early, when I arrived at work that morning. It was early, and a Friday, and this meant that it was the day we scheduled all the blood cancer appointments. As usual, the outpatient list was a congested stream of lumbar punctures and vincristine infusions, but for a small time, it was still what people call the calm before the storm. Aside from me and the nurse coordinator, only the outgoing night staff and the early shift of cleaners were in our section of the ward. Then the social workers came, and so too a volunteer, who set up a stepladder beneath another year's worth of Halloween decorations and began to take them down as swiftly as she had only a week or so ago put them up. Doctors filed in, and then nurses and more nurses. Then the receptionist came, as well as another volunteer with her pink apron and her ice-cream container full of cling-wrapped plasticine. One child arrived. And another. And then one more.

Ava had hair now, a short fair fuzz that she proudly decorated with a jewelled band. There was pinkness to her lips. She'd grown taller since her last appointment. 'Look at you,' I said as she twirled and grabbed at her nightgown like a ballerina.

Tom was having a harder time. You could see it on his face. His cheeks were puffed full of steroids and his head was shiny, hairless and pale. He pointed his thumb up at me. It was bandaged, a sign that the phlebotomists had already finger-pricked a vial of blood for the lab. 'It's Batman,' he said, thrusting his thumb back and forth until I registered a superhero crudely drawn onto the plaster with a ballpoint pen.

'It is!' I replied, and then I pointed to the sticker on his pyjama pocket—a red cartoon droplet with the words *I was brave*. 'Were you?'

'Yes,' he nodded proudly.

We made order on that ward. We grouped together the leukaemia kids, the brain cancers, the solid tumours and the soft tissues, and then within each of these categories, we grouped again, so that patients came through in cohorts. Ava and Tom were of such a cohort, each of them diagnosed just a month or so apart. They came in together. They lost their hair and their body size together. Everything about them—everything even down to their eyelashes—was at one time stripped not just to the bone, but also to the core so that almost all that remained was this wavering essence. It struck me how alike they once were—both stick-like and translucent, Ava swimming in a loose dress and Tom with his knobbly knees poking out of his shorts—and how different they suddenly became, how quickly Ava recovered. A month had passed—only a month—since her last appointment, but in that time, she had sprouted right back, regained something that had been suppressed for too long. Soon Tom would push through too. His body, having just expanded with steroids, would waste beneath the weight of the final round of intense chemo, but afterwards, in maintenance therapy, he too would reclaim at least some of what was once his.

Little Zoe, however, was different. She was new and in kindergarten. On the surface, she didn't yet have the appearance of one so sick. She still had her hair, for example, but on closer look, she was the clingy and tired one. She burrowed into her mother's arms even as Tom and Ava grabbed pencils and markers and seated themselves at the colouring tables. She didn't play with the plasticine like they did, nor did she roll out dinosaurs, tigers and stars.

Tom and Ava's mothers talked. But then they didn't talk. There was someone new, someone they hadn't seen before. They looked. They didn't look. They adopted softer, gentler voices. Ava's mother was the first to reach out. She said, 'I saw you in the car park. I thought to myself, "These two, please don't let them be for our ward," and then I came here, and you did too. I'm very sorry.'

Tom's mother joined in. 'What alerted you? What made you see a doctor?'

Zoe's mother responded with the same common phrases that had often circled our walls. 'I thought it was growing pains.'

'There were bruises.'

'She wasn't playing.'

'For a long time, she had a runny nose, but it didn't seem to go away.'

Zoe was about day fifteen, and although I had expected to see her, I didn't have her name on our scheduled list until the afternoon. 'Hi,' I said, and she looked at me and smiled shyly before pressing her head back into her mother's chest. She was a lot paler than she should have been, and I could almost tell just by looking at her that she would need a blood transfusion.

Zoe's mother, Catherine, seemed quiet. She had not a speck of make-up. Her hair was tied in a loose ponytail. She wore a simple pair of jeans and a t-shirt. No jewellery. Flat shoes. Everything was so unadorned. She placed her hand gently on Zoe's back. At university, I once learned that touch was the first sense to develop in the womb, and quite possibly the last to fade. Love was touch, and compassion was touch, and even if there were no words, even if everything was quiet but for a breath, touch could say all that needed to be said. *I love you. I love you. I love you.* And, of course, *everything will be alright.*

'I love you, Zoe,' Catherine said.

3

'I love you,' took on a whole other meaning on our ward.

I love you.

I need you.

Don't go.

Stay.

Be okay.

Motherhood was something else entirely. It was heightened, not a thing to take for granted or throw away. 'Come through,' I said to Catherine and Zoe.

'Can you tell me her temperature?' Catherine asked. 'Her blood pressure? Her weight?'

I said, 'thirty-six point nine,' and, 'good,' and, 'just under nineteen kilos,' and Catherine looked at me as though all the plates of food, and 'eat this' and 'have that' amounted to 'not enough' and 'next time more'.

'It's alright,' I said. 'She's doing alright.'

'Alright is alright. But still. I guess.' Catherine paused. 'She doesn't want to get up, doesn't want to move. This morning her brother helped her come to breakfast the way some people help the elderly cross streets. I'm holding her everywhere, even to the toilet and back.'

'Is this true?' I asked, directing my attention to Zoe.

She nodded and smiled, and then her face lit up. It was just a glimmer— the smallest moment.

'Are you thinking about your brother?' I guessed.

'Yes,' she said.

In the meantime, Catherine rushed about, unzipped a large canvas bag and pulled out a knitted blanket, a lunch box, a water bottle, a doll, a picture book and a small jigsaw puzzle, all of which Zoe ignored.

'How old is your brother?' I asked.

'Six. And I am nearly five.'

'Oh, you're close, like twins. I didn't know that.'

'Yes,' she replied. 'Next year when he is still six, I will *actually* be five.'

Catherine said, 'People do mistake them for twins.'

'You know ...' I told Zoe. 'My sister and I were close too. *Nine* years apart though. I bet your brother loves you the way I loved her when she was your age.'

'He does,' Catherine answered for Zoe. 'He really does.' Then she added, 'Why is she so sore?'

I looked at Zoe and thought of Emma in those early days: how still she was, how quiet and pained she seemed while her bones contracted—or *re*tracted for want of a better word—as the white cells in the marrow came under control. So much of what Catherine described was the same. I didn't consider at all that it could have been anything else, didn't think to check Zoe more closely, didn't make the connections I needed to make.

I said, 'You'll have to ask your consultant, but I do know this soreness happens.'

Zoe seemed tired again. If we weren't going to talk about her brother, she wasn't going to talk at all. Instead she lay on her pillow so quietly she could have just as easily been falling asleep.

Then the registrar came. She paused at the end of Zoe's bed, smiled at Zoe, looked at me, and said what I had already suspected to be true, 'Zoe's blood report came back with low haemoglobins. Will you please access her for a transfusion?'

'I have a headache,' Zoe complained. 'It hurts.' Then she started to cry. It wasn't hysterical tantrum crying, but long, slow sobs.

Morning came and went. And then lunch did too. I filled out theatre forms, slipped hospital bracelets around little wrists and little ankles, administered chemo, changed dressings, hooked Zoe up to an IV line and ordered the blood she needed. It was busy, pressured, the kind of shift where you need the scales to weigh a child but then someone—

a parent from one of the inpatient rooms, another child, a nurse—stops you in the corridor and asks for a bedpan or for a milkshake because so-and-so is not eating, or because something else happened, and by the time you're done and you turn around, the scales are gone, and in any case, you've forgotten what you need them for.

The clown doctors appeared. They were colour and slapstick, fits of giggles at a toilet rhyme. We all laughed along—even Zoe in her shy way, though it was hard to tell whether her laughter was real or the nervous sort. She wanted them to go. She wanted them to come. They tooted at her and gave out stickers. They bumped their faces into doors and walls. They sang. They played the ukulele. Captain Starlight came with her purple cape and a pocket full of balloons. A consultant visited. The clowns bowed out. Someone said, 'There's bingo in the afternoon. Make sure you tune in.'

And someone else said, 'She has cracks on the tips of her fingers and on her toes.'

The consultant replied, 'Let's take a look, shall we?'

And so it went on: this strange, unnerving mix of hospital and colour.

Then the music therapist came. Ava, in the bed opposite Zoe, took one look at the instruments the therapist was carrying—a guitar, some cymbals, a mini keyboard and a xylophone—and she said, 'Oooh, can I play the piano?'

In all this chaos, a peace finally settled. The therapist sat on Ava's bed, and for a little while there was only Ava on those soft notes, having been to theatre and back, having woken and eaten, having had her vincristine, waiting now for the dietician and for pharmacy, showing us Beethoven's *Ode to Joy* while the room filled with pending-Christmas and the sound of her voice singing, 'Mi-mi-fa-soh, soh-fa-mi-reh, doh-doh-reh-mi, mii-rah-raaah. Mi-mi-fa-soh, soh-fa-mi-reh, doh-doh-reh-mi, raah-doh-dohhh.'

We all stopped our talking then. Everything quietened. Zoe, across the way, seemed comforted somehow, less headachy. She didn't ask to play. She didn't laugh. But she no longer sobbed.

One of the nurses said, 'Hasn't Ava come a long way?'

The dietician arrived, and the pharmacist, and everyone talked all at once again about low-GI dinners and fasting times and, 'Here are your monthly meds.'

Then Zoe's blood finally came. I set it up along the IV pole. 'Can you confirm that this is Zoe?' I said to Catherine.

'Yes.'

'And when is her birthday?'

'Fifteenth January.'

'And can you read for me her patient number?'

'BD892351.'

The IV pole made a buzzing noise. The blood dripped through the line. As Ava and her mother readied themselves to leave, Zoe lay uninterested in books, in colouring, in anything. When Catherine offered up a lunch box of grapes, Zoe shook her head.

Ava skipped past. 'Bye,' she sang.

'Bye,' we all replied.

Catherine turned to me and said with a voice that seemed to need far more than I could give, 'Is everything going to be okay?'

I said the things we were taught to say. I said, 'Your child is unique,' and, 'Try not to think further than what's ahead,' and when that didn't seem to be enough, I added, 'I couldn't do this job if there were no it's-going-to-be-okays.'

'I have a headache,' Zoe repeated.

Catherine stood up, pumped antibacterial gel into her palms, sat down, stood up. 'Zoe,' she said, as though she suddenly understood her day had only just begun, 'I'm going for a quick walk. Two minutes max. Will you be alright on your own?'

Zoe nodded. Then Catherine left for as long as it took to walk the length of the fairy garden and back. I could smell the air on her, our synthetic grass, the windmills and even the music station. It wasn't the great outdoors, and it wasn't freshness, but it was *something*. She sat again at Zoe's bedside, picked up a magazine, and then put it down. She scrolled through the screen on her mobile phone, texted someone, left again, and returned once more with a cup of cold plain milk for Zoe, and a coffee for herself.

Zoe lay limp, the blood still dripping in. She didn't touch the milk.

Then her father came—Simon—dressed in a suit and looking as if he just left work.

Catherine pushed the milk and the container of grapes towards him. 'She's not eating,' she said.

'She'll eat when she's hungry,' he replied a little impatiently. For one brief but solid moment I remembered my father. There was a tightness around Catherine that I recognised. She and Simon didn't cuddle. They didn't greet one another. They were mechanical and short.

'I want my water,' Zoe said.

Simon put the milk aside and handed Zoe a bottle of water, which she sucked feverishly until it was all gone. 'More,' she said, passing the empty bottle back. While Catherine took the opportunity to give the milk another chance, Simon grabbed the empty water bottle and went to the nearby bathroom. As he held the door open with his foot, he filled the bottle from the tap at the basin.

'There's filtered water in the kitchen,' Catherine snapped across three sets of beds, but then when he turned back, she softened once more. Perhaps she sensed that he too was here, that this was his daughter, and that he had sat in that interview room, same as she did, and heard the news she heard, 'We know it's leukaemia; we just don't know what sort yet.' The doctors in that room would have asked her to stay, and him to go home and pray for the good cancer, and then later, after they dug around in Zoe's bone marrow, they would have come to them both with smiles on their faces. 'It's Acute Lymphoblastic Leukaemia,' they would have said, 'the good cancer.' As if such a thing existed.

Zoe drank the second bottle of water as though she hadn't drunk anything all day, and at the same time Simon opened his laptop bag and spread various electronic devices, a kaleidoscope, and even an old selection of DVDs out all over her bed. He plugged one of those portable modems into his computer, and then he put an iPad on the bed as for good measure. 'Want to watch a movie?' he asked.

'No,' Zoe said, but still he found something to play. He leaned back in his chair and as he stretched his feet out all the way across the base of Zoe's bed, the 20th Century Fox fanfare began.

Zoe rolled to her side. The blood finished. The IV machine beeped its high pitched, 'bip-beep ... bip-beep ... bip-beep ...' Zoe pulled her blanket up over her ears. There was something about her that wasn't quite right. She was headachy, thirsty, tired, but she had the blood she needed, and her energy shouldn't have been as low as it was. When one of the doctors passed by, I said, in as quiet a voice as possible, 'I'm worried about her sugars.'

'Yes, test them,' he said.

I grabbed the glucose monitor, told Zoe what I was about to do. Then I pricked her finger and dropped her blood onto the paper strip. The results were not good.

Catherine gave me a look. 'What? What's wrong?' she said.

'She needs insulin,' the doctor replied.

'She doesn't have diabetes,' Catherine snapped.

I said, 'Yesterday was her last dose of steroids.'

The doctor added, 'It happens sometimes. It's steroid-induced. She's likely to be fine again, but for the time it's an issue. It could be like this for a day or a week. It could be like this for longer. We're not sure.'

Catherine seemed so small. She said, 'I don't know what to do. I don't know anything about diabetes.'

The doctor replied, 'You don't have to do anything. We're admitting her into the inpatients section of the ward.'

Catherine nodded, and then just as quickly she shook her head. Simon had this faraway look—not worried, just faraway.

I said as slowly as I could, 'Catherine, I have to give Zoe some insulin.' I showed her the needle. It was the slimmest needle we had. 'I'm going to prick it quickly into her skin.'

'Zoe,' Catherine said, and Zoe turned to her, trusting her, the two of them wrapped in a maternal hug. 'Nurse Grace wants to give you medicine to help with your sugars. It's a needle. I'll be right here, next to you.'

As I injected the insulin, Zoe let out a great howl. Catherine flinched, closed her eyes.

'How long for?' she asked me later. 'What do I need to do? It's torture here... I can't do this... I don't understand leukaemia, let alone diabetes...'

'You're doing just fine.'

She said, 'I can't stay tonight. I can't. Simon is stronger. I can't handle this. It's too much.' She kept going, talking as if she was failing by leaving her child in her child's father's arms.

Simon, for his part, didn't exactly give Catherine the confidence she needed. When we turned back, he was right above us, large and looming, his legs spread a metre and a half apart. His hands were folded, but still filled to the brim with the laptop, the canvas bag and his DVDs— everything already collected and ready to be moved from Same-Day Care to the Inpatient ward. He took up so much space. He walked alongside Zoe as we wheeled her into her room, made funny faces and poked his tongue. He said, 'Zoe, is it okay if Daddy stays with you?'

Before Zoe could answer, Catherine repeated almost the same question over again. 'Are you sure you're okay with Dad being here and with me going home to your brother a while?'

Zoe nodded. 'Yes,' she said, but then just as Catherine readied to leave, Zoe added a meeker, 'I don't like this room.'

From that moment on, there was a sudden slowness to Catherine, as if she wanted to go and needed to, but couldn't. She cleaned the room, grabbed an antibacterial wipe and rubbed it over all the door handles, railings and bench tops like so many other mothers do.

She said, 'Simon, something is wrong.'

She said, 'Simon, I can't quite put my finger on it. I need to clear my head and I need to take a walk before I go home.'

She said, 'Zoe, I'm not leaving-leaving, not just yet, but I am going for a walk, and then I'll come back, say bye, and go home properly for the night.'

After Catherine left, Zoe picked up a picture book and flicked its pages. It was a cute book—all about a dog who wouldn't stop yapping. Something came alive in Zoe just to have it in her hands. She pointed to pictures and chatted to her dad about this dog, and for a moment, she looked stronger once more, better for having new blood and a shot full of insulin, and warmer too. She kicked her blankets off and bared her legs. I pressed buttons on her blood pressure machine. The cuff around her arm puffed up and went down. As I waited for it to do what it needed to do, I noticed—at least I think I noticed—a tiny pinprick mark on one of Zoe's calves. It was innocuous-looking, the kind of thing you don't quite register at the time but remember in retrospect. The blood pressure machine made its beeping sound. Zoe's dad stood on the bed. He pressed buttons too, but his were up high and on the TV screen. The image flickered from one channel to another. He was still wearing his shoes. They were black work shoes, and he had them on her bed.

My dad used to stand on Emma's bed too. The TVs then were also hooked to the ceiling. The bed controls never seemed to connect to the screens, and the actual remotes were always missing. Mum stood barefoot on a chair to switch from channel to channel, but my dad always wore his shoes.

＊＊＊

It had been a long shift that day: early when I arrived and late when the sirens blared their awful code blue.

One minute we were doing our normal, everyday thing, and then the next we were rushing through the corridors—all of us, doctors and nurses alike, rushing back to Zoe's room—and in our wake, Catherine, who had returned from her walk but had not yet gone home, was pushed clear out of the way. Sirens that once rang for my sister now also rang for Zoe. She was in and out of low consciousness, a vomit bowl of black blood strewn across the floor beneath her. Catherine surged all the way forward. 'Is-this-what-happens-is-this-normal-is-this-chemo? You're-not-going-to-lose-her-are-you?' One, two, three, four doctors examined Zoe. They scanned her body top to bottom. Catherine surged again and pointed to what used to be the pinprick mark but now looked like a bruise.

'What is that?!' she shouted. 'WHAT IS THAT?!'

Dopamine. Insulin. Sugar. Heparin. Saline. Antibiotics. Fluids. Someone took a swab, and someone else said, 'ICU is on their way.' We were loud, and we were scared.

'What is it!?' Catherine repeated with this shrillness in her voice. 'WHAT IS IT!?'

For a few seconds, she stood on the outside of everything, shaking and watching from the sidelines as if someone had just stretched a fluorescent ribbon that said 'DANGER' and 'DO NOT CROSS' from one side of the room to the other. She stood behind the line, shivering, and all I could do was the same thing someone once did for me: I took her hand and brought her forward. Then I picked up the picture book that was on Zoe's afternoon-tea tray, passed it to Catherine, and said, 'Do what you can to keep her awake.'

4

It was early when I arrived at work, and late by the time I ran my usual stretches of coast. Physical pain didn't seem to have the appropriate effect on me. It beat and beat, but no matter how hard I pushed myself, or how fast I ran, the stitch that came and went and the soreness that weighed down my legs never quite tempered what Zoe had just faced or what that reminded me of, and so, I ran like I always did, and I thought the same thoughts I've had ever since Emma and I were small—*if I run harder ... if I run faster ... if I reach that fisherman before he reels in*—and although logically I understood that my running never made (and wouldn't make) a scrap of difference to the outcomes of the world, I kept right on going until I felt I might collapse, and then I ran one kilometre more, and it was only in that last kilometre, in that final stretch, that my thoughts began to shift back to me. There were other conversations I needed to have, other worries beyond the hospital. I touched my stomach. Embryo, what a strange word that was. Em-bry-o. Probably Latin. Or one of those Greek words that ought to roll off my tongue but doesn't.

If ever there was anything to put the brakes on.

I was powdery. There was ocean salt on my eyelashes, on my lips, on my skin. I waited until my breath evened out, and my sweat too, and when I was calm again, I stood swamped by the immensity of the sea. The beach was dotted with swimmers, paddle-boarders and other runners who nodded and smiled as I stood still and they flew past.

And then, two things:

At the edge of the whitewash, there was a seagull tangled in a fishing line, one leg bent in a knotty sling while the other struggled to take the weight of its body.

At the edge of the whitewash some distance further along, there was a family: Nate, his wife Al-i-son, their toddler child and a baby not more than two months old.

Oúte arhí o télos: that's what my mother would have said. It was one of the few things she was certain of, and I would hear it in her voice, both in Greek and then in English as if the repetition of languages made everything all the more authoritative. 'Gracie,' she used to translate for me, 'There are no beginnings or endings, only moments to look forward from, or those we look back to.' This was how she comforted herself when Dad left, and also at the hospital. Time was a flattened, stretched-out, never-ending string; this happened, then that happened, then that led to this. Everything overlapped not in a neat sequence of births, marriages and deaths, but in befores, nows and afters. *Before we had kids. After you were born. About the time your father left. In the holidays. At school. When I finish my study.* And then, *before Emma fell sick,* and of course, *after.*

I never saw our story so simplistically. Time wasn't at all chronological. Time was Emma and the paramedics and Zoe and the sirens all at once. I carried time like a sphere inside of me, a history as inescapable as the ground I walked on. When we were little, Emma and I dug a seep-hole at the edge of our lake. It occupied us for ages. We used our hands to scratch at the earth. We piled the excess sand to the side in the same way bulldozers manage complex construction sites. We became dirty, itchy and sun-dazed, but then, right when we were about to give up, water surged through the bottom and rushed into our well. That was how time was to me. Like a seep, erupting forth. Like little bursts of knowledge that never quite went away. Like the words my dad used to say, like 'up the duff' and 'knocked up' and 'belly full of arms and legs', and the way those words returned to me. Life twisted like the fishing wire that was wrapped around the seagull's leg.

I looked at that gull as he hopped away from the waves and the danger. 'How did you get yourself into this mess?' I thought, and 'Will you sit long enough for me to unwrap you?' But I knew as I stepped closer and it hopped back that it would not trust me enough to let me help, and that more to the point, I was unlikely to shift past my own fears, and so

I wondered also if this was going to be one of those moments I looked forward from, or back to, or if instead it would one day rise like seeping water and erupt through me all over again.

I wanted to shout at the top of my lungs: *I'm afraid. I'm not afraid. I wish… I long… I'm twenty-nine now but I can still see your patient number on all those bottles exactly as they were when I was thirteen and you were four. I can still see the instructions—take ONE tablet ONCE per night on an empty stomach—and the irony of the words, KEEP OUT OF REACH OF CHILDREN.*

What if I can't be the kind of mother that the other mothers are?

It climbed from my core to my throat. It lodged like a rusty coin.

Embryo. Tumour. What a poor comparison. They weren't the same. If left to grow, one signified life and the other death. And yet that's what it felt like, as if I was equally out of control. As if I had something to fear.

I put my feet into the ocean's foam and angled my body so that if by chance Nate did glance my way, all he would catch was the back of me. The water had a chill. The current now flowed in and then out, and as it did so, the sand tugged beneath my soles. It felt tactile, but then it also reminded me that the only time that really mattered was nature's time, and the time of the tide, and the time it would take for the child within me to grow.

I looked back over my shoulder towards Nate and his wife, and then again towards the seagull. It was tied and twisted, and I wondered how long it had suffered and how long it would take for that other time—the time we have left—to tug and topple it into the sea.

Be brave, I told myself. *Help it. Try.* I stepped forward. The seagull hopped back. I thought about taking my shirt off, stretching it between my hands and using it like some kind of sheet to create a stable nest between the bird and me. I thought also about asking Nate to help. And then I thought about the conversations we'd later be forced to have.

'The thing is, I *am* married,' Nate would say.

'I don't know what to do,' he would say.

People say that time heals wounds, that you must give things time, or that in time everything will work out. When Emma and I dug for that seep, we dug for the heart. We drilled towards the well. We looked for water, and when we found it, we were as shocked by the rush as we were by the iciness. It was cold and fresh, and we couldn't help but put our hands in to touch the clay beneath it. In my pool, at my core, I was still that girl, yearning for touch, wanting sensation. When I looked back towards Nate, I saw my father and what he did to my mother. I saw the lies I told myself and the truths I omitted. Nate had a wife. He used to touch me as though we belonged to one another, but in the end, he was really just the-man-I-cheated-with-for-too-long and the-man-who-didn't-want-to-think-about-pain. We matched, I guess, because I must have been the-girl-who-accepted-and-understood. I was hungry and yet I didn't care to be nourished. Nate gorged, and I scavenged, and even then, even with the cold hard knowledge that we had reached the end, even with the image of his proper, honest-to-goodness family—the boy jumping in and around the ocean and sand dunes, Alison dressed in virgin-blue with the baby snug in a carrier over her belly, and Nate holding both Alison's hand and their oversized beach bag spilling with oversized toys and towels and other family things—even with that freshly etching into my memory, even then, my longing for his touch was both distressing and familiar.

I thought I was strong. People used to say it to all of us. 'Oh, you're so strong. You're an inspiration. You make me see what's important.'

I touched my stomach. I couldn't yet feel it. I couldn't yet see it. I wasn't nauseous. I wasn't anything. But it *was* there, growing, its cells dividing. I blinked, and already its cells had split. I blinked again, and the cells doubled, and doubled again.

The seagull stood not even a metre away. It faced the horizon in the same direction as I did. I was always so timid, always so afraid. *Be brave,* I thought, *plunge over it. Help it.*

5

At home, I lingered by my letterbox just that little bit longer than I needed to. It was well past dusk, but the sky was pink and pretty, and the breeze was still warm enough to draw everyone outdoors. People were walking their dogs and watering their lawns. Rosa and Katerina— the neighbourhood widows and biscuit-makers—chatted beneath the frangipani tree out the front of Rosa's house. The old man from a few doors down pulled imaginary weeds out of the cracks in his driveway. He often did this, often weeded the same path he had weeded the day before. Sometimes he watered a single pot plant until a flood spilled over and his wife came rushing to take the hose away, but that evening, he seemed content just to keep tidying whatever he was tidying. Across the road, at Cole's house, a young boy bounced his football again and again. He was a cute thing—skinny, fair and about six or so—but he wasn't from around our way, and so although he seemed happy enough to be visiting and playing, he also looked out of place. He had this shyness about him that reminded me of myself during the months my sister spent in hospital. Cole sat on the paving behind him with her university notes on her lap. I waved, and she waved back, and because I sensed the same discomfort I sensed in the boy, I called, 'How are you?'

'Good,' she said, but then she made one of those so-so signs with her hand. The boy said something to her then, and she nodded and stood up, brushing dust and dirt off the back of her pants. She tousled his hair, and then made her way a small distance diagonally across from him where she quickly clapped her hands together twice as if to say, 'Come on then.'

On cue, the boy pumped a strong kick of the football towards her. When Cole marked it, the boy smiled and shouted, 'Good one, Coley. Good one.' Cole kicked back. The boy readied himself and then caught the ball fair and square in his hands. 'Did you see that?' he yelled. 'Did you?'

Cole nodded, and they kicked—kick-to-kick—for as long as it took me to clear the junk mail and read the catalogue specials. Then Cole said something or another, and as the boy nodded, she drew both sides of her cardigan around her and made her way inside.

The boy widened his playing circle so as to make use of his new-found space. He punched the ball into the air and took a flying mark. Then he flicked his fringe and pulled at his socks before thumping the ball across the courtyard. 'GOAL!!!' he shouted, doing this roaring crowd noise, jumping up and down like he'd won the grand final itself.

'William!' Cole called through the doorway. 'Your mum wants to know if you read your book for school.'

'Three goals four, twenty-two,' William replied, kicking a ball across two sets of driveways.

'William! Your mum said your teacher set you a reader for the weekend.'

'Four goals four, twenty-eight!'

'WILLIAM!'

'Four goals five, twenty-nine!!'

Cole was not normally the kind of person to do large amounts of cooking, but that evening, the distinct smell of roast floated all the way from her house towards mine. 'WILLIAM!!' she shouted.

'IN A MINUTE!!'

A minute passed and then another too, but instead of following what Cole wanted him to do, William crossed the street and kicked his way into my front yard. He bounced his ball on the paving bricks, bouncing it up and down, bouncing it as loud and as exaggerated as the rhythm of a drum.

'Excuse me,' he said. 'Are you a nurse?'

'Yes,' I replied, but because I was in my exercise gear and not my uniform, I asked, 'How do you know?'

'My aunty told me.'

'Your aunty?'

'My Aunty Coley,' he said as he bounced the ball another two, three, four times. Then he added, 'Did you always want to be a nurse?'

In that moment, I thought about my life before Emma's sickness, and after, and how easy it was to choose nursing once I had spent all that time in a hospital. 'I don't know. I guess. What about you? What do you want to be?'

'I'm going to be a footy player when I grow up, and also a scientist. In case I get injured.'

'Wow. That's a great plan. Better make sure you do your reading then, like your aunty wants you to.'

He nodded. Then I nodded. Then he nodded again. As I flicked through my mail, he kicked his ball—a big torpedo—back towards his Aunty Coley's house.

Cole called to him, 'Come on, William. Come and help. Come on. Come inside.'

William followed her voice into the house, but then no sooner had he disappeared, he returned again carrying two glasses, juice splashing over the rims. Cole tailed him, not far behind. She balanced a bright blue picnic blanket with dinner, cutlery, napkins and plates.

'Sit,' she nodded, as she set everything down.

William placed the drinks on the picnic blanket and wiped his hands against his shorts. Then he sat, just like his aunty had asked and began to eat so quickly that he was licking his plate clean and wanting seconds before Cole had even lifted her fork.

I opened my bank statements, the electricity bill, the telephone account and then a 'with compliments' slip from the GP which was attached to the scrap piece of paper I had left behind during my last appointment. On one side of the paper, in the GP's handwriting, was a list of five obstetricians that had space to take me as a patient, and on the other was the name of a clinic that would make it all go away. I don't know how long I looked at this sheet.

William finished seconds or maybe even thirds. Then he stood up, grabbed his football once more and started kicking and booting goals over the top of Cole's head.

'William, I'm eating!' Cole said. And then, 'WILLIAM! I mean it!

You're going to get in trouble!' And then finally, 'Oh my god, William, you actually cracked the window.'

She was strong and stern, and she took me exactly back to the day Emma and I broke a shower door ourselves. We had been banging it open and shut, over and over, sliding it from the left side of the railings to the right when one thing led to another, and suddenly we were fighting, and a great split appeared across the glass. It just appeared as if an invisible someone had marked that door with crayon. We stopped arguing quick smart after that, but our mother's voice still tore through the walls, 'You should have been more responsible!' For weeks, there was a rainbow exactly where the crack filled with steam. It was such a magical stripe. I would stay in the shower for an extra length of time just to look at it.

Dad used to say it too, but before he left us, and before Emma became sick. 'If anything happens to Emma, I'm holding you responsible.'

We used to spend hours curled on the couch—Emma and I—every evening reading a bedtime story, the two of us on the couch with her legs poking out of her nightie, straight out, not reaching the floor. Those bare toes. And the way she listened to my slow vowels while she slurped her milk through a straw.

William across the road now sulked his way inside. Cole looked up at the crack, and also back to her plate. She reached out and pushed her meal away. Then she stood up, poked her head into the doorway, and gave the boy a hug.

I unlocked my door, hung my keys on a nail above the bench.

I could be good at it. I had the skill. I could raise a child. I could be just as calm as Cole seemed to be.

It was like an echo, this fear I had. Like the time Emma called through the hospital's underpass and waited for her voice to bounce back. Or when the stroke patient I nursed on my first practicum told me she could hear herself speak twice: first in her head, and then again later, out of her mouth. She would think the word, and then the word would begin. She would touch her forehead and then her lips. 'Here, then here,' she would say. 'Here,' tapping at her temple. 'Here,' pointing to her mouth. Like the mountain nymph in my mother's stories, cursed to repeat only what was already said. Like the sonograms we recorded of our patients' tiny fist-like hearts.

As I piled my mail onto the kitchen bench, I looked once more at the list my GP had sent, and I thought of all our patients at the hospital, and in particular, the echoes that would forever keep track of their health and the other echoes too—the late-effects of their cancers and chemotherapies—and I found myself returning to the words Harriet had said before we all left our lake town—*take care of your heart*, and *don't look back*—and I wondered what noises I would hear if I finally made it to an ultrasound myself, and what whooshes there would be, and what thumps. It wasn't that I didn't want to be a mother; it was that motherhood came with no guarantees. How could I predict whether I would be the kind of mother my child would need? How could I dream of the things other mothers dreamt of—teeny-tiny clothes, first words, first steps—without also dreaming of the sirens that once took my sister to ICU, or without remembering the way in which my dad retreated from us all and left?

I pictured my mother then, thought of her, and before I knew it, without really thinking about it, I was dialling her number on my mobile phone.

'Hi love. How are you?' she said without skipping even a beat.

'Fine,' I lied. 'I'm fine. What about you?'

She told me about the holiday she had planned, her teaching and the student of hers that had trouble with her English. Then she added that she was thinking … just maybe … she might go back to study some more, a postgrad perhaps. Now that she felt capable of such a thing.

I said, 'Mum,' but she kept talking.

She said I ought to come over this weekend. She had zucchini for me, and tomatoes, and soon there would be crop full of blackberries—not quite the same as the wild ones that used to grow by the stream near her old village, but good enough.

I said, 'Mum,' hearing myself that second time, a beat or so later.

'*Ti eínai*?' my mother said, reverting to her Greek, as if Greek conveyed a pause that English didn't. 'What is it?' she repeated. 'Are you okay?'

But then my speech seemed to loosen, and I lost my nerve. I was speaking and listening, and I wasn't sure what to say, and so I found myself returning her 'okay' without having had the conversation I needed to have.

An echo: that's exactly what it was. My thoughts bounced back like Emma's voice on that underpass wall. *I don't want to be alone if something goes wrong.*

Scared: that's what it was. I was scared of going it alone, scared of our genes, scared that all the awful things would somehow repeat.

It was dinnertime, but I didn't feel like dinner. Instead of chopping vegetables on a wooden board or flicking through recipe books, I grabbed a mug, poured in some milk and stirred a spoonful of Milo just like I used to when I was small. Right at the last moment though, after I had opened the microwave door and placed the mug on the turntable, but before I closed it up again and pressed the buttons on the timer, something came over me. All those years and I had never thought of the microwave. I thought of mobile phones, my parents' arguments and x-rays. I thought of BPA plastic and the lining inside cans of tuna and baked beans. But I had not thought of microwaves. In one quick and irrational swoop, I unplugged and heaved this same microwave to the garage. If it would've fit, I would've put it in the bin. In the kitchen, I sopped the sponge full of warm water, and then squeezed the water right out. I wiped the crumbs and dust that had accumulated on the bench beneath the base. It seemed like such an oversight.

I don't want you, I thought. *I don't want to be a mother.*

And yet, maybe I did. If I was throwing out the microwave ... if I was boiling milk on a stove instead of in that radiation ... if I was protecting me and him-or-her-or-whatever-the-baby-is, then what did that mean?

Instead of microwaving the milk, I stood over a saucepan. I stirred each and every chocolate Milo dot until they all dissolved away. I poured the finished drink not into the mug I had originally intended to use, but rather, specifically, into the old scalloped teacup that had once belonged to Harriet. My teacup. The teacup I often drank out of when Nate still visited.

Outside again, I drank my milk for as long as the cup was warm against my fingers. It was quiet and dark by then, but not as dark as I would have liked. In fact, the sky actually disappointed me, and I wondered if the night-time back home at the lake was still as black and as awash with stars as when I was small.

I placed my Milo next to me. The china echoed against the paving bricks. Across the road, the front door clicked open and then it clicked shut, and when I looked up, Cole was unwrapping an ice-cream for William. She sat him on the same blanket they sat on before, and she pointed to the sky, and then while William licked his vanilla cone or whatever it was, she said, 'Look at the bright one. Can you see? All the way high?'

He was in his pyjamas—singlet and loose shorts, hair all wet as though he had just come out of the shower. In his left hand, he held a box of biscuits—Tiny Teddies or those mini choc chips. He angled his head to the sky and said, 'Where?'

'Where?' I thought in that cynical way.

'There,' Cole said.

But William had already moved onto the next thing. He pushed the box towards her, bit at his ice-cream and said, 'Did you know the cassowaries at the zoo are getting a new exhibit?' And then, 'Can you open this?'

Cole tried but couldn't. 'It's slippery,' she said.

William looked at her, and also at me, and then he ran from his house across the road to mine.

'William!!' Cole shouted. 'Look left and right!'

William said, 'No cars, Coley.' And then he said, 'Hi.'

'Hi,' I replied.

He passed me the box. They were chocolate chip, the smallest size. The cardboard was open but the plastic beneath was firmly glued at the top. I tore it apart, handed it back, and as he finished his ice-cream, he scooped out five or six biscuits with his sticky hands.

He said, 'Did you know the cassowaries at the zoo are getting a new exhibit?' all over again. And then he nodded towards the biscuit box and said, 'Do you want some?'

I shook my head, 'No thanks,' I replied while he ate by the handful, crumbs spilling all the way back to his place.

Later, after Cole and William had long-gone inside again, a car flashed its orange indicators out the front of Cole's house, and a man who looked a bit like Simon from the hospital and enough like William to be his dad walked to the door with little more than a child's backpack and a small suitcase. He rang the doorbell, and then the two adults—aunty and brother, or aunty and brother-in-law—stood on either side of the threshold, talking and pointing to here and there and upstairs too.

I couldn't really hear what they were saying, but when the man left again, so soon after arriving, he walked briskly to the car, and he did not look back, not once, not even to see William with his fingers and face pressed against the upstairs window. It struck me how silent and civil this separation was, and how ghostlike William had become. The glass seemed cold against his skin. William watched the tail-lights on the car, and as I watched him, something rose in me, something small and long ago. I wanted so much to pull him from that window and wrap him in a soft blanket. I wanted to say, 'Don't worry. Whatever is happening, it's not because of you.'

6

When Emma first fell sick, guilt dragged me through time all the way back to the games we played, the things I said, and even the things I thought, as though *thinking* was all it took to bring her cancer into being. At night, I used to repeat phrases like, 'Every cell in your body is filled with light and love and good health,' and so long as I touched the wooden headboard behind me or stirred the chocolate dots out of my Milo, the thoughts and places of my past—the day I taught her to play tennis, for example, and then told her she was dead, then buried, and then finally a ghost whenever she missed the ball—seemed placated and smaller than before. 'If anything happens to Emma,' I used to think. 'I'm holding *you* responsible. *You're* the responsible one. *You* ought to know better.' Guilt exhausted me. It blanketed me into sleep in the same way a current blankets a weakened swimmer beneath the tide. As soon as I lay my head on the pillow, I relinquished myself, because there, in that other darkened place, guilt did not exist.

Guilt now was of a different sort. It didn't wash over me or drag me into any kind of sleep, but rather I tossed and turned in that clichéd way. I got up and paced. Late at night, I even took to a printed photograph—a selfie of Nate and me—with a spent staple. I scraped out his face, and then mine. I ripped at the image, exposed the threads of paper beneath. It seemed luxurious, this kind of guilt, as if I *could* think about it, as if the worst that could happen was never really the worst at all.

Instead of sleeping, I brought out my paints. I wasn't accomplished—I chose to study nursing over art—but I did like the calmness that settled into my body. All I painted was colour. All I wanted was the rhythm of the brush moving up and down. It was silence I was looking for, a reprieve from the noise of Nate and little Zoe and the sirens that made me not want to return to work.

The lights across the road were dead out. 'It's not your fault,' Nate had once said, and his words sliced through me, blade-like, but in a necessary way.

And now?

Either I have the baby or I don't.

Near midnight, I grabbed my car keys. I drove around the block, once, twice, three times, unsure of where I was going or what I planned to do. At the traffic lights, just outside the bar Nate so often performed at, I watched a man stumble off the curb. He was drunk and young, and when the lights turned green and we all took off, he seemed to trip and fall like a broken pull-toy. I was sitting at the next set of traffic lights when the thought began to surge. 'You hit him. You did.' Old scripts came rushing. Old obsessions and repetitions. I actually had to turn back, but when I drove past again, I found him completely unhurt, crouched and fumbling with his shoes. He was fine and calm, rocking on the ground, trying to tie up his laces.

I, on the other hand, was not calm. My heart was thumping, my head hurt, and I felt hot. I pulled over and sat on the side of the road, behind my steering wheel while other cars passed and beeped their horns.

Then, when I no longer felt the pulse of my heart through my clothes, I drove to Nate's house, and upended the council bin.

That's what I did.

I drove up onto his verge and tipped a bin full of rubbish so that the contents spilled along the road. A newspaper hurtled across my windscreen. Grainy pictures of a plane crash and debris stuck to the glass. Before I knew it, I was at the end of his street and he was out the front, standing amongst all that mess.

His house was warm and lit, lights gleaming. And then, she was there too—Al-i-son—with their baby swathed in pink and wide awake in her arms. Nate bent to collect the rubbish while Alison swayed on the kerb, absentmindedly caressing the infant's cheek.

When I returned home, I leaned over the steering wheel and sat in the driveway for a long time. The landline rang across the road. The lights flared open. Through unshuttered windows, I saw Cole make her way across the kitchen. She stood with the phone to her ear. When she hung up, she drew out a dining chair and sat at the table with her head in her hands.

WHEN I THINK OF MY CHILDHOOD

7

Before my sister's leukaemia, the colours of summer were olive and orange, and the leaves, which were narrow, crunched underfoot. We lived in a lake town equal distance from the cities to the north and to the south of us. It was an in-between place, the kind of community that attracted miners and construction workers, farmers and artists as if they were all one and the same. We had tuart trees. We had swamplands. We were a brackish town, estuarine—magical as far as I was concerned—but the tourists often bypassed us on the way to somewhere else. To a lot of people, we were just the roadhouse on the highway, a quick stop for fuel or for a meat pie or a toilet break, but for those who knew, we were part of a national park—a system so large we spanned hundreds of kilometres of forests, camping grounds, walk trails and wetlands. The tourists who did come, they came for the whole of that park. They came to swim and fish in the ocean twenty minutes south of us. They came to camp or to photograph our birdlife. They came specifically for the thrombolites that lined our lake. The tourists painted these thrombolites. They took pictures. They stood on the viewing deck and listened for the bubbling that sounded from below.

At school, we learned that our thrombolites originated from the earliest forms of life. Our teachers taught us about the microorganisms that created them, the processes of photosynthesis and precipitation, and the oxygen that arose as a result. Where once thrombolites covered the Earth, now they occurred in just a handful of places including the four square-kilometres on the eastern shore of our lake. They were delicate, dependent on a fine balance of calcium, groundwater, light and a saltiness that belonged to the ocean but remained trapped in the reservoirs of lakes like ours.

I liked the lake. I liked how it changed. The lake was difficult to know. It was forgotten, tucked away. In the summer, the air was dusty and stringy, and it left a film on my fingertips much like the beach, only drier and more powdery. The thrombolites looked sun-bleached and reef-like. They were life-giving and oxygen-producing, yet when the heat came, they could have just as easily been bone. Sometimes the lake was so shallow the thrombolites shimmered as though they were crystalline. From a distance they looked domed, like brittle-salted skulls.

My sister and I often went to the lake. Emma was my shadow, my audience, always following me, always copying. She was my twin, nine years apart; that's what my mother used to say. We didn't look like one another. We didn't share the same birthday. We had different personalities. But we were always together, always connected somehow. We stomped our footprints along the walk trails. We peeled at splintery bark and scratched love hearts and stick figures into old tree trunks. At that lake, the two of us were equally as Australian as we were Greek. We were the eucalyptus of the land in which we were born, but we were also the limestone of the memories and myths my mother had carried from her home.

Sometimes we sat together—Emma and I—and I shared with her our mother's stories of Persephone and Demeter and the meadow that cracked open into the Underworld, or else of Orpheus and Eurydice and their song of sorrow and instructions to never look back. But other times, I held on to Emma, and warned her of real-life quicksand and the ghosts of actual sisters who long ago set sail to the centre of the lake but never returned.

I was full of storytelling. I inherited villages from my mother and local histories from my father, who had in turn absorbed the kind of schooling that began with lieutenants and admirals and ended with names like Peel, Herron and McLarty. He told me the lake was out of bounds—not for swimming, not for walking, not for playing. It was a forbidden place, the kind of place that swallowed children in muddy sand. That's why we came—Emma and I—because we weren't allowed.

Even the twigs on the shore looked like bones. They were amputated fingers no longer of flesh, a buckled shin bone, a broken rib. I was scared of the lake, deep down. It gave me the impression we were alone, but if I looked closely enough—under leaves, in shallow roots, on the sand—I saw ghosts of another sort: tracks in the earth, sharp bird claws, insects trapped in large golden webs. There were snakes too—whole colonies of them—wriggly baby dugites soaking up the sun. I shouted at Emma, 'Run! Don't fall behind!' I wanted her exactly by my side where I could protect her. Emma was as happy and as scared at the lake as I was. It was our secret place, the place we went to when things weren't quite right.

Aside from the now-and-again tourists, there were only ever a handful of people who shared the lake with us. We saw them from time to time, scientists recognisable by their jars, birdwatchers with their binoculars, and workers marking ribbon around the trees. When they were there, *we* were the trespassing ones. They didn't like Emma's noise or the way she played. 'What a little handful,' they said, 'and don't go touching the rocks!'

Harriet and Samuel were the only ones who never made us feel that way. They were the newcomers to our town, talked about and gossiped over. Emma and I knew them well before we had even met them. Harriet was an 'artist' and a 'home-wrecker', and Samuel once 'worked in a bank'. They were 'tree changers', who had 'run away together', and who were now 'starting up some kind of olive oil, greenie arts market thing'. This was what people had said, what I had heard. I closed my ears to all those words and imagined instead that Harriet and Samuel were the grandparents I always wanted but never met. I used to watch them on the jetty or along the trails or where the picnic tables and car parks were, and I often wondered where they were from, and where they now lived, and if their home was near or far. I wondered also if they did grandmotherly and grandfatherly things, and what it would be like to have the kind of grandparents you could visit for milk and cookies or for a quiet spot to be looked after and watch TV. They say you know yourself through what you are not, and what I yearned for, even then, was a grandmother.

Mostly though, I found Harriet only at the lake and only sometimes. Never on a regular schedule. On the jetty there, she busied herself, just like my mother might have, with some kind of sewing work, or else she sketched our lake inside her notebook while Samuel took photos of the same through telescopic lenses. Every now and then Samuel brought a small portable stereo along. He hung it from a tree and played chirping sounds, and as the birds responded to his call, he turned to Harriet and said things like, 'So the doc thinks I ought to avoid seeds.'

And she replied with a firm but teasing, 'No more tomatoes then?'

Samuel wore a big red cardigan. Even in the heat of summer he was all wrapped and buttoned up. He played his stereo of calls, and the lake filled with birds. Sometimes he nodded towards Emma or to me, and he said, 'Do you know what that bird is called?' ... 'Or that one?' ... And 'Can you see the shelduck there?' Other times, he shared a picnic and a quiet space with Harriet. He called her 'Arete' or 'Reti'—which reminded me a little of the Greek name my mother had given me—and she looked up over the top of one of her pencil sketches or even over the needlepoint she sometimes brought with her, and then they both chatted about something or another and picked at sandwiches before returning to their individual worlds that always seemed threaded together.

What I liked about them both was their softness. My family did not have this same softness. We were as loud and as mechanical as speedway drag races, the sound of bottle tops being opened and the television that always seemed to be humming in the background. My dad and his friends talked cricket and played pool. They drove down to the beach and fished and came home with buckets full of gutted whiting. They sat around bonfires, drank 'one for the road', and shifted conversations almost simultaneously from the results of the one-day test to visa restrictions and the migrants who were stealing their jobs.

Samuel didn't speak like my father and his friends. He was quiet, even in an argument. 'No,' I once heard him say to Harriet. 'I'm not doing it. I'm not sitting on an exchange every five hours for half-an-hour a pop. I won't put you through that.'

Then it was Harriet—something and something and something— until Samuel spoke again. 'It'll make me angry,' he said. 'If my body needs a machine to do what it ought to do automatically, then my life is as good as done.'

'Please,' Harriet said.

And Samuel insisted, more firmly than before. 'When the time comes, you give that chance to someone with a bit of life left.'

This was how they argued—like a tennis match. She spoke first. Then he did. Then it was her turn again.

In my house anger never softened so quickly. Where I came from it lasted days and days and went on no end. Anger reminded me of the moths near our porch light, the Christmas carols that drifted in from a neighbour's house, and the smell of someone else's barbecue. Anger was my mother pulling her clothes off their hangers, the clang of wire against the metal rod, and the contents of her wardrobe in the usual three piles: one for the bin, one for the poor, and one to keep. It was the blotchiness of emotion on my mother's face, the sound of my father's car turning into the driveway late at night, and the daylight which came before any of us had the chance to sleep. On those mornings, my mother put the cushions back on the couch and my father rubbed his shoulders and neck from a sore night spent on the lounge-room floor. 'Our relationship is miserable,' my mother said over cereal and a hot cup of tea, and my father replied that it had *moments* of misery, only *moments*, and that there were good times too. He touched my mother. He rested his hands on her shoulders, kissed her crown, and then left for work as if there was no hole in our pantry door.

Those were my school holidays. They were sticky and humid: the kind of days where my mother slammed an unwashed bowl with remnants of Weet-Bix into the sink, and the only thing I heard was the terrifying crash of it splitting in two.

I took Emma to the scrub. The air was freer there, and lighter. We scratched our names into the earth. I pointed out a beehive. I said what my mother often said to me, 'Make sure you get an education, okay. A proper one. Never put yourself in a situation where you depend on a man.'

Then I said, 'Emma, I love you. One day, we'll get out of here, okay?'

I looked at Samuel and Harriet, at the love between them. My parents—they never held hands.

8

By March the lake was a feathery landscape, a scratched pencil sketch lacking strong lines, a mess of scribbles and scraggly sticks. Our town felt cracked, like peeling skin. It ached for moisture and for the comfort of that first wet day. The hours shortened. Butterflies hatched, and little orange flares burst briefly into the sky.

School slipped into an endless cycle of lessons and routine. Most days I caught the bus with the blonde girls, the netball players, the strong-shouldered swimming champions. I was the one with the inward smile and the mother who filled my drink bottle with water instead of cordial.

Autumn was for folk and ballroom dancing. We filed into the assembly area and swirled around the centre circle in do-si-does and awkward slow rhythms. We heard the words, 'Forward. Together. Side to side. Step ... Back. Together. Side to side. Step ...' and when we changed partners, the boys—not all of them, but enough to fix this in my memory—crept their hands towards our buttocks and our budding breasts, and then called us tight if we complained, and loose if we didn't.

Soon the days began to chill. It happened quickly. All of a sudden, there was dew when we woke. Things seemed rich with green again. After school, I took Emma to the lake. The water levels were deeper than in the summer, but still shallow enough to see the thrombolites. They glowed golden beneath that surface. The lake filled with swans and ibises and plovers. Everything was glassy. I had things to tell Emma, to warn her about. I said, 'Boys are not nice,' and old Samuel, who was there again with his red cardigan and the portable stereo of bird recordings, overheard and laughed.

Harriet pointed low in the sky. 'Look!'

'Butterfly!' Emma squealed.

'Moth,' Samuel corrected.

It made me cross. I didn't quite understand why, but so much of me wanted him to be wrong. 'Then why does it fly during the day?' I asked defiantly.

When the butterfly-moth came to rest on the stem of a plant, not far from where it took off, Samuel said, 'Watch the way it holds its wings flat. That's what makes it a moth. A butterfly carries its wings like sails.' He stretched his arms to show us, but then his elbows had a frailty about them, as if the very action of moving his limbs and joints hurt him more than he expected.

Emma played on the outskirts of that lake, amongst walk trails and the bush. The sand was springy beneath her feet, yet she stood with good posture and spread her arms up and down as though she was the one taking flight.

'Now that's a butterfly,' Samuel said. He turned to me, 'So what's so bad about the boys then?'

'Lots,' I replied. 'They think they're the boss of everything.'

Autumn cooled. Soon there was a bite to the air: that irritability we felt when we were still habitually wearing summer clothes when it was socks we needed, or a jumper.

My parents bickered about dirty clothes left on the laundry floor, what to make for dinner and whose turn it was to bathe Emma or to help with my homework. My mother complained that she always seemed to be left with the dishes, and Dad cuddled her while her hands were immersed in soapsuds. He cuddled her from behind, and she cringed away. That's how he hugged her: from behind, above, around, over her shoulders, always when she was cleaning, and always when he was late or when his mates were over for drinks and a barbie. He was chatty and full of dreams, my dad. Mum was quiet, cutlery clinking along a stainless-steel sink.

Sometimes Dad pinched her bum. And sometimes she threw his things against the walls. Travel clogged up the television. As did the cooking shows. If they spent time together at all they spent it staring straight ahead, the flickering of a TV screen between them. They were in Vietnam, for example, Mum eating fish smoked inside a banana leaf. Or else they skied on New Zealand slopes. Dad flicked the channel to our other regional station. He found the sport. He found the crime scenes. He upset my mother, set her off again.

I drew pictures of how it seemed to me: caricatures of my father coming home late with news and lots of it, comic strips with speech bubbles full of money and job offers and too-good-to-be-true opportunities. There were no words for my mother though, just Dad: 'Aw don't be like this, love, come on and talk to me.'

I drew the mornings that followed their arguments too: our Saturdays spent mushroom picking. Emma and I foraged in the ground the way other children foraged for chocolate eggs. Twigs snapped beneath my mother's feet. I drew sunshine through the trees. If I had known how, I would've pencil-sketched the sound of my mother's breath, walking and not-talking. Instead, I drew a small warm memory in amongst the repetition of everything that hurt: Mum frying hot mushrooms for our dinner, and Dad drinking his port.

Autumn was Easter, and Easter reminded me of prescribed forest burns and the heady smell of eucalyptus oil and rain on a hot road. At home, there were red fabric dyes on the kitchen bench and Palm Sunday crosses in a vase above the mantelpiece. My mother never seemed overly religious to me, but during Easter she was everything her Orthodox parents would've wanted her to be. She was austere and reflective, ceremonious, steeped in tradition. She plaited buttery dough into *kouloúria*, lit a prayer candle, and prepared to dye at least a dozen eggs. We cut old stockings into tubes. We wrapped these eggs with a fern and the nylon tube, which we knotted shut and tight, and then when we were done, my mother lowered the eggs into a large stockpot of water and paint. It stunk up the house, that boiling dye smell. Between that and the burning off outside, the air was inescapable. My mother sang in a language I barely knew. The more she fought with Dad, the more she retreated to that other self of hers, that Greek self, the one belonging to a family and a culture far away. In the evenings, she shone the red eggs with oil. We picked the best of them—Emma and I—the prettiest, the ones with the sharpest patterns and the stencilled prints of bottlebrush leaves. These were the eggs we wanted to crack on Easter Sunday.

We went to church. We travelled out of town. Dad was happy to drive and happy to take Mum, but whenever I thought of church, I thought also of Dad's workmates opening their wallets for their share of the Red Rooster family packs they could only get in the cities and bigger towns nearby. I thought of my mother too, the red-and-white drive-through and the smell of chips going limp at the base of her passenger-side chair.

At church, there was a low hum, a chanting that rolled into hours and hours and several days' worth of us standing and kneeling and crossing. We were anointed with oil, we sang, we stood with candles and collected flowers from wreaths. Church was hard on Emma—she was fidgety and tired—but when the clock struck midnight on Easter Saturday, she grew just as excited as the rest of us. We filed outside with our candlewicks glowing orange. We wore our best clothes and most polished shoes, and while the priests led us in their familiar and comforting repetition of 'Christós anésti', passers-by stopped to stare. Sometimes I folded my head down and snuggled right into Dad's arm space. Other times, when I didn't want to need him so much, I used my fingernails to form wax spirals onto my candle, and then also onto Emma's. Dad licked his lips of chicken salt and grease, and Mum snarled at the stink. She gave up meat and dairy for Lent. She made bean dips and lentils for dinner. But there he was, Dad, eating a pineapple fritter and chicken out the front of our church.

In the car, on the way home, Mum held our still-lit candles at arm's-length and took care not to let the wax drip on her skirt. In that all-encompassing darkness those tiny flames were beacons. They were good luck, she said. They were health and wealth and love. Dad wiped the foggy windscreen with his hand. He reached near my mother's legs for a piece of chicken, and when she jerked those candles back, he winked and said, same as he said year after year, 'They're gonna think we're the occult or something.'

I turned towards my window. It was steamy and tempting. I drew with the pad of my index finger: love hearts at first, then flowers, then treble clefs. I wrote 'help' backwards, so it was large and legible for anyone looking in. The night outside was empty. The letters opened a portal into vast darkness. It stretched before us, infinite. I wiped my drawings clean, and the blackness grew. Dad put the demister on. Every now and then a reflective road sign flashed some light, but mostly the road and the trees and the sky were one and the same.

At home my mother used the flames to make the sign of the cross above the entranceway that joined our carport to the kitchen. It comforted me, that cross. It made me feel like nothing bad could ever happen so long as the sections of plaster at our door and on the eaves above were blackened with our smudgy Easter smoke. She said, 'Step inside using your right foot first.' Right was luck and left was not, but all too often Dad walked in the wrong way around. He did it on purpose. He liked the look on my mother's face, those silent words that passed between them.

Inside our house, chicken soup simmered on the stove, an avgolemono made with stock, lemon, egg and rice. My mother placed the church candles in a narrow vase, and while she checked on our midnight dinner, Dad carried a sleepy, or sometimes sleeping, Emma to bed. I turned the TV on. It was music at that time of the night, always music, which we soon overlayed with the sound of the exhaust fan, our murmured chatter and the slurping of soup.

On Easter Sunday, our house was thick with the smell of slow roasted lamb. There was a stuffing: a village recipe of soft rice and fried liver. There was a cabbage salad too: a tart coleslaw dressed only with salt, oil and lemon juice. Mum basted the lamb and Dad brought his friends— always his friends and their wives in those drinking circles, always Dad with a beer in one hand and a cigarette in the other. He wasn't normally a smoker, but he did have a just-in-case stash of cigarettes that he kept in our garden shed. On those festive Easters, the smokes surely appeared, and when Mum complained, he simply told her to 'Relax love,' to 'let go,' and 'she'll be right,' because 'it's un-Australian not to have a good time,' and 'besides, no-one ever got cancer or heart disease from one or two.'

Amongst those friends and on those festive days, Dad turned Mum into something special. He spoke about her customs and all the things from her stories to the foods and flavours that her cooking offered, but when dinner came, Dad and his mates ate as much cold chicken as they did my mother's lamb. The Red Rooster boxes were as bright as our dyed eggs and as white as the image left by the ferns. Dad drank and smoked. He wiped his hands of fat and grease. Mum picked up a painted egg.

We all did. '*Christós anésti*,' we said, bumping our eggs together and cracking for tradition and for a winner. The shells dropped onto our patio bricks like broken china, and while Emma and I swept them up again, the adults gossiped and chatted. I heard my mother say, 'I met Harriet finally. At the bakery. She's lovely.'

I weaved in and out of Dad's wafting smoke. I blew my breath through the V of my index and ring fingers and pretended I was smoking too. In the evening, my sister stayed up as late as I did. We lay with our faces and bellies skyward, both of us stretched on our trampoline, showered and dressed in our fleecy pyjamas but with our feet bare and our cheeks flushed. Emma had her yellow bear and I had my music. We cracked yet another pair of eggs, our third or fourth for the night, and as I giggled a competitive I-just-beat-you-*Christós-anésti* kind of giggle, I turned to her and I noticed—I was the first to notice—her eyes didn't sit quite right.

I said, 'Some people have never seen these stars.' I didn't know the constellations save the Southern Cross and the Pointers, so I created connections of my own and the stories to match. 'Can you see them too, Emma? All the things I can?'

'See them, Emma? Those ones from our flag? Those ones Emma. Draw a line down from that cross. Do it, Emma, draw it, draw another one from the Pointers. See where they meet, Emma. See it? That's the South Pole, and if you fall to the ground from there, you will always find your way south. Did you know, Emma? Did you know that's true? Do you believe me, Emma?'

'No,' Emma said. 'You can't fall from the South Pole.'

'You can,' I said.

'Cannot.'

Late in the evening I stole one of the light-coloured beers Mum allowed in the house and Dad said tasted weak as piss. I pulled the tab and sipped at the fizz. It was awful and sour. 'Can you really see all the things I can, Emma?' I asked again, pressing my pupil right into hers, so as to examine the swirl of movements and the floating changes that happened with each blink. I told her I bet she saw double: twice as many stars as me.

9

When winter came, the lake was deep and full of birds and bulbs of light. I longed for a storybook snow with a storybook Christmas, yet our winter was quite unlike the ones I read in my novels or the ones my mother told me about. Our lake did not freeze over and we did not make snowballs or wear puffy coats. Instead the days wavered between sunshine and rain: never a predictable pattern, and often a mixture of both. In the mornings, we opened the curtains to filter in as much sun as possible, and at night, we shut them again to trap the warmth inside. When the darkness settled, it was as empty as outer space. Sometimes the rain lit up this darkness. Sometimes I sat between the heavy backing of the curtains and the cold window and watched this rain beat against the world.

It was cold in the winter, and windy, and yet our house had a warmth and an attention to detail that was absent in the summer. Things were cleaner, more aromatic. The persistent tumbling of the drier comforted me, as did the sound of my mother's ironing press. We moved freely together, kindly. There was a calmness to us. We were interwoven and seamless. I drank a warm cup of milk. I wore my tracksuit pants and a singlet. I read my books by our fireplace and Emma coloured in while our mother sat on the couch threading embroidery cotton through the tapestry stencils that her own mother had sent to her. It seemed to calm our mother, this cross-stitch art of hers. On those winter days she gave us small gems, gifts of her memory: a sailor uncle who brought home dolls and snowdomes from his various ports and washed her with the same desire to cross oceans, a beekeeping father who drove her all the way to Athens to organise a passport and a mother who packed for her a wooden chest of all the things that ought to reconnect her whenever she needed connection.

Now and again, winter after winter, our mother showed us what was in this chest: crafts our grandmother had handspun or handmade herself; fine crochet; tablecloths with delicate flowers embroidered in the corners; blankets and rugs woven out of course goat's wool. We moved from ourselves to each other and then back to ourselves again. We were quiet and the stories came and then we were quiet once more. Mum went to the kitchen to chop cauliflower for our dinner, to the laundry to take the final load out of the dryer and then to our bedrooms to put away our clothes. Emma returned to her colouring once more, markers strewn now across the floor, and I sat myself right up close to the glass of our dying fireplace, book in hand again, reading but not also reading, looking intermittently at our mother's half-finished tapestry resting on the arm of the couch.

Then my father came home. He appeared out of nowhere, and before I knew it he was right in front me, opening the fireplace door and poking at the embers. 'It's just about out, you little shit.'

'Ow,' I said. 'Close the door.'

'Come on,' he said. 'Come help with the firewood.'

Out past the carport Dad handed me a log for each hand. As the wood dangled precariously in my grasp, he laughed and said, 'You're a fairy-touch, you know.' He laughed again when I found splinters beneath my skin. Dad removed these splinters with a flame-blackened needle. The needle hurt, and he yelled at me to 'Sit still, sit still ... and stop wriggling.'

Mostly we ate thick wintry casseroles or tubular pasta layered with bolognaise and cream. On the wettest, coldest days my mother baked bread. Sometimes the loaf was plain, which disappointed me, and other times it was her mother's doughy village recipe: a bread filled with feta, which I ate warm and straight from the oven while the cheese was soft, melted and salty. Bread like this came with more stories of the childhood my mother left behind, but in these stories, she was not the

'Mary' she currently went by. Instead she was 'Marigo', who pronounced her *g*'s all mixed with the *ye* of 'yellow' or 'yearn'. When I said 'Marigo' too, I felt it way down deep in my throat. It was a passionate sound, like desire, or anger, or hunger, but it wasn't a sound my Australian-born voice made with ease. It brought to mind images of my mother waiting on the tarmac for the plane that would bring her to Australia, Greek music in the background, and streamers too. I thought of her, eighteen and full of hope. As 'Marigo', she sang and waved her family goodbye, but as 'Mary', she was not what I had imagined she had once been. 'Marigo' danced on tables, while 'Mary' folded laundry and waited for my dad to walk through the door.

That last winter, the winter just before Emma fell sick—food filled my memories. It was good food, and plentiful. There were glasses of milk for Emma, and big trays filled with tiny snacks. There were dried apricots and cucumbers and perfectly rounded cookies, all of which were accompanied by the sound of my mother begging Emma to eat. Most nights at dinner, Emma wanted her yellow bear. She wanted to colour. She needed a bangle. 'No,' my mother said. 'Finish your food.'

My father came to the table but not before he switched on the TV.

'It's yucky!' Emma said. Or 'I don't want it.' Or 'I'll do my eating if I have Rice Bubbles.'

Dad turned up the volume.

Emma repeated, 'I want Rice Bubbles.'

The sound of the television.

The sound of my mother: 'You're not getting Rice Bubbles.'

And Dad: 'Oh for fuck's sake.'

And then: 'Don't swear in front of the kids.'

The television.

My mother again: 'Turn it down please.'

And finally, Dad, 'If you'd all BE QUIET, I wouldn't need it so loud.'

I ate in small mouthfuls. Each bite was heavy and large. Mealtimes dragged on. My mother pushed lamb or sausages or slow-cooked beef into Emma's mouth, and Emma sat there, not chewing, not swallowing, but storing this food inside her cheek.

All too often I was the one who took Emma out of there. I walked her to the bathroom and scooped the mashed food from her mouth. I brushed her teeth and showered her and wrapped her in a towel. We chose pyjamas or a nightie together. We read stories. She lay on her bed and made a space for me. She said, 'Gracie, is the bogeyman real?'

'No,' I replied.

'How old are you when you get dead?'

'I don't know,' I said.

'And if Mum and Dad die, do we get new ones?'

'If Mum and Dad die, we'll be orphans, but I will still look after you no matter what.'

Then she giggled. 'Grace, there's two of you.'

'What?'

'You have four eyes, two noses, two mouths and two heads.'

'What are you talking about?' I asked, pressing my lashes right up against hers. The wobbliness in her pupil was even more pronounced than it was at Easter. There was even a swirl. I said, 'Emma, we should tell Mum.'

'No!' she panicked. 'It's okay. It's better. I promise. I made it up.' She rubbed her eyes.

'Muuuum!' I called.

'What?' Mum yelled, but she never actually came.

Emma held her yellow bear. She had a dry cough, a scratchy cough. It punctuated the air at irregular and unexpected intervals. She coughed herself to sleep, and then she snored. She sweated. Her face looked flushed, not rosy, not pink, but as though she had just run to the lake and back. I shifted her head this way, then that. I lifted her onto her pillow and used the tip of her sheet to wipe the beads of moisture that sat above her lip.

'She'll eat now, OR NOT AT ALL.'

Arguments circled around and around: same topics but different words. I stirred every last chocolate dot out of my Milo. I wiped the dishes before the commercials finished. I counted to one hundred, knocked on wood and hoped nobody spoke.

During those evenings, Dad ordered me to come turn the volume up, and Mum snapped at him to find the remote himself. I never watched television with my parents. I didn't like being in the same room. Instead I read near the fire where there was just the crackling of logs, the sound of rain and a distant football commentary which was easy enough to ignore. By that fireplace, everything came to me as if heard beneath a blanket. The rain made things quiet in a way. It muted the other sounds. It added a kindness, a softness. 'For what it's worth,' Dad said, 'dinner was nice,' and, 'Thanks,' and, 'Pass us the remote, will you?' He switched between channels. 'You had a good day?' he asked, though he never lifted his gaze from the television screen.

In the meantime, I stayed in my space. I read my books. I drew. I found another splinter on my thumb. It hurt when I poked at it. Dad called out, 'What are you doing over there?'

'Nothing,' I lied.

There were so many splinters over the winter that Dad took to leaving a pin on the mantelpiece. It sat there in the same way wooden spoons and wooden canes sat on top of old-fashioned fridges. I grew hyper-vigilant, often with my back to the fireplace door, often with my body facing outwards. I never told Dad when I had splinters, and I hardly trusted him even when there were none. If I so much as fell asleep at the hearth, he jolted me awake by pricking my skin with a pin. He loomed large over me. He laughed, and his laughter hurt almost as much as the pricks themselves.

Sometimes, after all the lights went out, my parents' whispers turned into shouts. 'Shush,' my mother said. 'You'll wake the kids.' And then, 'Shush,' again before the yelling unravelled like a ball of string.

'You're not listening. You're not LISTENING. YOU'RE NOT LISTENING,' my father said over the top of my mother's voice.

'Who were they for?'

'NO-ONE.'

'There were strawberries, cream, two cans of cool drink and ...'

'YOU JUST KEEP GOING AND GOING.'

'... fancy dark chocolate. That's not something you buy just for yourself.'

'Let it go,' he said, his voice lower this time.

But she didn't let it go. 'Who ate them?' she wanted to know. And, 'Why were there two drinks?' It went on for the longest time: those strawberries and what they meant; and Dad, and his sarcastic words about jumping to conclusions being registered as an Olympic sport;

and Emma, of course Emma, that sudden raspy cough no one seemed to notice but me.

Then something cracked. Something always cracked: a piece of wood, a drinking glass, a plastic Barbie, a door. The house went quiet. 'Congratulations,' my mother said. 'Well done for that.'

There were reasons not to visit the lake in winter. Winter was beautiful, silvered and glassy, but it was also dangerous, cold and muddy. The snakes were hibernating, slow-moving, full of poison and too cold-blooded to get out of the way. Yet when I lay in bed and listened to all those slammed doors, rising arguments and awful silences, the wilderness made perfect sense. I pushed my flyscreen out. I left Emma in her bed. I went on my own, and I was not afraid.

At night, the thrombolites glowed as if they too were lunar. Even immersed in water, they gave the lake a graveyard quality. It was gothic, and I was ghostlike. On the other side, the paperbarks and tuarts looked shadowed and rickety. Some had the dieback that rotted them from the inside. Their branches clawed, not to the sky, but down to the earth. I knew from science class that these branches were bending for water, that they could barely find it, and that there was no stopping what was to come. When the moon was low and bright, and the clouds moved slowly, those trees looked crippled and drawn from a horror movie. A nocturnal animal scurried near my feet. I jumped, and for a moment wings surely beat at my cheek. I was scared, and then I was not. I was cold and wet. A fine drizzle settled on my cheeks and on my nose. I grew so familiar with that landscape. The real horror, I thought, was the one I had at home.

Back outside my house, my foot gave way amongst uneven ground. In the darkness, I made out the imprint of my father's boot facing the street. I looked for it actually—that tread in the dirt. That's how I knew the fighting was over with. My window gaped open—a big wide clue to my absence—but I never got caught. I clambered in, shut it, and pretended I had never left.

I felt damp beneath my covers. My heartbeat grew loud and quick. It was a rush—always an excited, just-got-away-with-something rush—that kept me from sleeping. I was busting and hungry and all sorts of other things. I passed my parents' bedroom on the way to the toilet.

The moon shone through their window. It lit almost everything. My mother slept on her side. The space next to her was flat and empty. The whiteness of the cupboard somewhat reflected the moon. There was a fist-sized hole on one of the panels, another head-level, wrist-deep hole which splintered both the paint and the wood.

10

Early in the spring I turned thirteen. The sun shone. The sky was blue. There were kookaburras, magpies, and the sound of Emma singing, 'Happy birthday dear Grac-eee.' We shared a picnic—Mum, Emma and me. We did not go to the beach down south like we might have had Dad come along. Instead, we went to the lake where we balanced on fallen tree trunks and walked the length of the jetty. Deep in the water, schools of tiny fish darted around, reeds swayed, and a green moss-like substance crept out from beneath a stony ledge. We lay flat on the weathered wooden planks, dipped our fingers in and stared at the reflecting and rippling clouds as if we faced the sky.

Mum told us old myths about why there was winter and why there was spring. There, on the lake, we learned again that for half the year, the Goddess Demeter lost her daughter to the depths of hell, and that in those months, Demeter, whose job it was to tend to the harvest, grieved so much that the crops withered and the sky grew dark. Then spring came, and Demeter was allowed to have her daughter back again. The sun came out, the grieving stopped, and the grounds grew thick and fertile once more.

We learned words too, Emma and I. *Káto*, our mother explained was 'down', and *káteva káto* was 'come down', and all of this was related to the Ancient 'katabasis', which implied some kind of 'descent' or even 'a trip down to the Underworld', and, 'Here's the thing, Grace, listen now, *katálava* means "understood". Do you see? Do you understand?'

Spring was for lovers, and lovers liked the lake as much as Emma and

I did. Around us, the parklands, the nearby vineyard, and the boardwalk were all dotted with people—not the scientists or the birdwatchers, but regular, touristy people, coupled together, kissing and cuddling.

We bumped into Samuel and Harriet all over again. They were walking along that jetty, and when they saw us, Harriet smiled and waved. Samuel carried his binoculars, and Harriet a picnic bag. I imagined she had her sketchbook in that bag, cheese sandwiches, some kind of craftwork. I looked at my mother, and caught her looking back at Samuel and Harriet, looking at them in the same way I sometimes did.

'Bet they keep you busy,' Samuel said to my mother.

The adults all laughed, and Harriet looked at my mother and said, 'I've met you before, haven't I?'

My mother nodded. 'At the bread shop, I think. How is your market coming along?'

'Good,' Harriet replied. 'Not long now and we'll be up and running.'

Emma and I scrambled to the walk trails. We rolled our jeans up and took our sneakers off. Baked sand broke against our feet. 'Crunch,' Emma said. 'It crunches.'

We stepped forward, not knowing that each step was also a tick on the clock closer to the space where no words would ever form. There we were, drawing pictures in that sand—hearts and butterflies and birds. Our mother walked beside us. She held our drink bottles, and every now and then, she asked if we were thirsty or tired. She handed these bottles back to us. Everything was perfect. Everything was all that it wouldn't be in a few weeks' time.

Spring consisted of the eight weeks *before* and the four weeks *after*. We were destined to return and return and return to my birthday, and then to all of September and October searching for that first warning sign. 'Is it here?' 'Here?' 'Here?' A rash happened, a runny nose, a dream. Nothing was significant. Later, every small gesture, every word, every action held meaning. We looked back for that meaning. What we wanted was some semblance of an order, a story. We were hungry for the thing that clicked and made the rest make sense. But nothing made sense. Spring was disjointed; it was without sequence.

We were at the lake. We were walking home. I held Emma's left hand, and my mother held her right. The bitumen felt warm beneath our soles but not yet burning hot. Somehow, somewhere, we had forgotten our shoes. Emma's feet looked small in comparison to mine. Her nails were polished pink, but her toes were black from the dirt. It got to me, this blackness. 'Mum,' I said, collecting a twig from the ground, because collecting a twig was virtually the same as knocking on wood. 'Mum,' I repeated.

'Yes?' she replied, but I never actually told her what I needed to say because Harriet was suddenly behind us, huffing and puffing and carrying our shoes.

And then, there they were, my mother and Harriet, talking and not stopping. I could hear them—my mother asking all about Harriet and Samuel and how they met and how long they had been together and what the secret was to long-lasting love. I could hear other things too, an aural escalation and de-escalation of bonds they had in common: Harriet sewing and my mother gardening and Harriet telling her that she had migrated too—from England though—when she was small, and that her grandfather was Greek, just the same as my mother was.

'Grace, Emma, come, are you listening?' my mother said. 'Harriet here, her grandfather was from my *geitoniá*, my neighbourhood.' She used to do this, my mother. She used to say Greek words alongside their English translations, a kind of double-speaking, a repetition.

'We're from the same parts,' she said. 'Harriet's family is practically from my *méri*.'

In the evening, Emma pulled my mother into a hug. 'I love you, Mummy,' she said. 'Mummy, I love you.'

'You're beautiful Emma,' my mother replied as she drew Emma a bath. 'You're so special. I'm so lucky to be your mum.'

I dressed in my pyjamas. I flicked through the crisp pages of the books my parents had purchased for my birthday. I read snippets in random chapters: Heidi was locked away in Frankfurt; Meg begged God to spare Beth; and Sara, in a short, tattered frock, mounted two flights of stairs to an attic, worlds away from the princess she used to be. When I finished flicking pages, I scribbled with my new set of pencils. Yellow came in *lemon*, *straw* and *chamomile*. I had eleven greens. If I wanted to, I could have sketched every nuance of the lake. I was happy. I was warm. I hardly noticed that Dad was now so rarely home.

Then my mother said, 'Emma, what's that?' And: 'Emma, get out of the bath!' And then, in a voice shrill enough to hurt my ears: 'Gracie! Gracie!'

'WHAT??' I shouted back.

'Get the antihistamine. It's in the fridge. Gracie, please!'

It all seemed so urgent, so bossy. 'You're beautiful,' I thought, as my mother's voice caught up with me. 'Special.' In the kitchen, I grabbed the bottle of medicine and dosed Emma carefully according to the instructions. I thought—and I remember this clearly—I thought, 'I want to be special too.'

Emma had a rash on her back: a flat pin-pointed, dark-dotted rash unlike any rash I had ever seen before. Outside, the bottlebrushes were all in bloom. In the moonlight, the leaves had a dappled effect near our flyscreen. We didn't yet know the word *petechiae*. We didn't need to. It was spring. We were *all* itchy. We were *all* suffering. It was simple: the bottlebrushes were flowering.

My mother pushed the medicine cup to Emma's lips. I sneezed. Mum pulled the plug and let the bathwater swirl down the drain like the whirlwind still to come. She patted Emma dry and wiped the mucous from her nose. It was clear and thin, not like a cold, different in a way, and persistent. She said, 'Gracie, you're clogged up too, is that right?' and when I nodded, she slammed the bathroom window shut. She reasoned, 'They did say the pollen count was high.'

Some nights Emma's voice came to me through a blanketed dream. 'Mum, I'm wet,' she said, 'I'm wet, Mum,' and then the shower was running, and my mother was stripping pink sheets off a pink bed and bundling a load of laundry while the clock on my bedside glowed half past four.

Emma said, 'I want to sleep in your bed, Mum. Pretty please? Pretty, pretty, pretty please?'

She was just outside my room, dressed in last year's pyjamas with the hem five-eighths the length it used to be. Mum was there too, shifting the wet tangles of Emma's knotted hair. Emma wrapped her arms around our mother's neck, and Mum nodded, patted, took her in.

'Tomorrow can we paint a picture for Dad? Can we? Mum? Please.'

She painted a lot of pictures, Emma. She painted houses, and people in front of houses. She painted rainbows and flowers and fish in the sea. She set herself up on our dining table, and laid out a splash cloth, several wads of paper, a brush and six pots of colour. There was water in a jar. There was an empty egg carton, a makeshift palette. Emma mixed colours, red over blue and blue over yellow, but in the end, everything— the water, the cloth, her paintings—swirled into an inky bruise. She called out, 'Mum look! This one is of you sleeping in bed, and that one is Daddy driving in his car.'

The washing machine beeped. Mum stuffed pyjamas and other bedclothes into the barrel of the dryer. 'Have you finished your cereal?' she asked, and when Emma failed to reply, she redirected her voice to me, 'Grace? Is Emma eating?'

I kicked Emma from beneath the table. It wasn't a hard kick, just enough to indicate I'd rather be reading. 'Eat your food.'

'Ow,' Emma cried.

'Grace!' Mum shouted. 'Don't hit her.'

'I didn't,' I said.

Mum came to check on Emma's plate herself. 'Shit,' she said, 'Emma, you've hardly eaten anything.'

'Swearword,' Emma replied.

'It doesn't count if I find you're not eating,' my mother said as she cleared away a plastic bowl of a breakfast gone soggy. She poured Emma a glass of milk. Then she grabbed herself a gossip magazine. 'Drink up,' she said. 'Come on, quickly, drink up,' she repeated as she sat next to Emma and read over a two-page magazine spread of celebrity weddings, iced cakes and pastel bouquets.

Emma shouted, 'I'M NOT HUNGRY!' and Mum flicked the page so hard it ripped.

11

Spring was when I decided to learn how to boil an egg. Every morning I had it in me that I was to start the day with a perfect, soft-boiled egg—one with a firm white, no gooey bits, a runny yolk, an orange ball with no green ring, no cracks, no blurring of boundaries, a shell that peeled away without pulling at the actual flesh—but the eggs I cooked were either soggy or set like rubber. It became yet another obsession. I threw away more eggs than I ate, but still my mother stocked the fridge full of cartons knowing most would end up in the bin. She was good about it. She didn't say, 'Here, let me,' or 'I can cook it.' Instead she let me do what I needed to do.

I buttered a piece of toast and sat down, but when I sliced my egg, it collapsed, oozed. I began again, boiled water, buttered toast, sliced another egg. I started a journal. I wrote: *me v soft boiled egg. Attempt 32. Egg wins again.* I stood over the stovetop. I heard my own voice, 'If I get it right this time, if, if, if, everything will be okay.'

Eggs, Milo, wooden headboards and counted steps began to swarm my head. Then the egg cracked, and the albumen snaked through the water. My mother looked at Emma. She looked at me. It was as though everything was set in slow motion.

'Oh my God,' Mum said either that morning or some morning so close to it, that it could've been the same. 'My dream.'

Before I understood what was going on, she was at the stove with me, and then at the table with Emma. She was hugging us and hugging us and kissing us as though we were lost to her. She held Emma especially close. She kissed her forehead. She said, 'I love you little one.'

And when I said, 'What was it? What did you dream about?' Mum shook her head.

'I love you,' she said. 'I love you. I love you. I love you. Both of you. You're all that matters.'

'I love you,' she said. All day long, 'I love you.'

'Was it bad?' I asked later.

'Was what bad?' she said, as though her brain had already made the decision to forget.

'Your dream?'

Her face fell. She told me then in her slow and quiet voice that she and Dad had grown apart, that they'd been talking, that they thought it might be best if... She made it sound so civil and considered. He hadn't left yet, she explained, but he wanted to, and it was inevitable, this thing that was going to happen. She said she woke up worried in the night and when she fell asleep again, she dreamt of Emma. 'Something was awfully wrong,' she said, 'And I was lying by telling her it would be an adventure.'

In the days that followed—before school and after—my sister seemed to play less and less. She slept later, went to bed earlier, coloured, flicked through picture books, and sat on the floor with a box of Barbies, but when I said, 'Come to the lake Emma,' or 'I'll take you outside,' she shook her head and refused to stand. Sometimes she called out, 'Muuuum, carry me!'

To which my mother replied, 'I'm not your servant. Use your legs.'

In the spring, I hated my sister and I loved her. 'Can I take you to the lake?' I asked.

'No.'

'Do you want to play?'

'No ... Muuum, carry me. My knees hurt.'

Then Emma dropped a crayon and when she bent to pick it up, she flinched and yelped as though she had caught the same pain that once stopped Samuel from stretching his arms like wings. 'Ow,' she said. 'Ow.'

And then a little later, 'Carry me?'

I held her on my hip. I took her to her room, to her colouring, to wherever she wanted to be. Early one evening my mother caught me with my eye up close to Emma's eye, and she wanted to know what the hell I was doing. She said it like that, 'What the hell are you doing Grace?'

I said, 'Can't you see? Her eyes aren't right. *She's* not right.'

She said, 'Oh for goodness sake.'

I said, 'Please Mum, look.'

So she looked, really looked, but she didn't see what I saw. 'There's nothing there Gracie. It's not nice what you're doing.'

I tried again, 'Mum.'

'Grace ...'

'Mum!'

'I said, stop it.'

'Mum,' I pleaded. Because I knew. Deep in my stomach I already knew.

Then the bruises appeared.

Mum took Emma's clothes off for her bath and ...

It was Halloween. The doctor could fit her in the very next day.

The next day came, and I went to school. I was scared. I was thirteen and I had never been more scared in my life. If I solved the page of maths problems before the bell went ... If I ate my sandwich before the netball girls ate theirs... If I came top of the maths leaderboard ... If I. If I. If I.

After school, I caught the bus. I ran from the stop all the way home. My backpack swung left and right the whole time, whacking me, winding me. My feet burned even in their shoes. My legs buckled beneath me. I ran faster than I had ever run before. I had a stabbing stitch, but I told myself not to stop. If I stopped something awful would happen. If I stopped ... Don't stop.

My mother met me at the door. 'Gracie,' she said, calm as anything.

'What is it?' I replied, darting my eyes from her to Emma and then to the three overnight bags by the door.

And then she said it; I don't think she remembered, but I did. She cuddled Emma. She grabbed our bags, and she said, 'Come, Emma, let's think of it like an adventure.'

12

It was a red car, a small car—at least it felt small, the way we were shut in like that. My mother drove, I sat in the back with my books on my lap, and Emma held her yellow bear tight in her arms even though the rest of her appeared soft. Before we knew it, the trees shrank in size and number, and in their place, houses popped up, all of them the same uniform, unimaginative beige. I didn't speak to my mother. I avoided her reflection in the rear-view mirror. If her voice so much as cracked, if I saw worry in her eyes, I would have surely crumbled. Emma was so little, strapped to her seat, showered and dressed as though it was seven in the evening instead of four. Her head drooped in a drowsy half-sleep. Her legs dangled down. Her favourite ballet flats, the red ones with the sparkles at the heel, hung off her toes. Every now and then the sun hit at the sparkles, and tiny disco balls of light splashed across her face and mine.

As we drove, I looked inside the windows of the cars we passed. Everyone else seemed chattier and happier than what we were. Even the rhythm in which they moved their bodies suggested they were all listening to the same radio station. We listened to nothing. My sister rubbed her eye.

'Are you girls alright?' my mother said, and as she looked into the rear-view mirror, I caught a glimpse of something that I didn't quite understand; it was in her pupils, as though her pupils had trapped a small and frightened animal in there.

At the hospital, Mum carried Emma, Emma carried her yellow bear, and I carried my books and all three overnight bags. We walked slowly to the edge of the car park and then down through the underpass. The bags pulled at me. They were heavy, lumpy and awkward. Emma had slept and woken, and now she wore this bewildered, 'Where am I?' look on her face.

Mum said, 'Honey, maybe you should walk?' but Emma shook her head and gripped at my mother's neck. We walked from one end of that underpass to the other, and when we came out just in front of the hospital, my mother asked again, 'Emma, walk now?'

Emma nodded this time and, as she wriggled down away from my mother, I began to convince myself that there was actually nothing wrong. Emma stopped, turned back and faced the way we came. 'Echo!' she called through the tunnel and onto the brick wall that was the base of the car park.

'E-cho, cho, co, o, o,' was the sound that returned.

'Did you hear that?' she said, pleased with herself. She did it again. 'Echo!' and her face lit right up when her voice bounced back.

At the elevators, I said, 'I want to go home,' and I meant it. My mother unzipped her handbag and pulled out a Post-it-note full of her scratchy handwriting—*white cell count* and *high* and *Ward 3, downstairs, to your left*. Then the elevator came. My heart sped away.

It felt weird, disorientating. We came in on the ground floor, but then we went *down* to 'three'. There was no 'one', nor a 'two'. Everyone else seemed to go up to 'five' and 'six' and 'seven'. It messed with my head, this numbering. It made me wonder why we were different. Why were we hidden so low in the depths?

Level three was yellow. The lights were bright and artificial. There were no windows, just long blank corridors. It was cold, and pungent with mopping and antiseptic and the kind of food that was steamed and broiled and served with plastic gravy. Emma gripped at my mother with one hand and me with the other. We turned a corner. We stood in front of two opaque electronic sliding doors. 'Oncology'. 'Haematology'. 'Transplants'. 'Total care unit'. That's what was written in neat blue writing across the entrance. 'Oncology', I knew meant cancer. 'Transplants' were transplants. And 'total care' made me think of people who no longer got out of their beds. 'What's *hAYmatology*?' I asked.

'*HEEma,*' my mother corrected. 'It has an *EEma* sound, but it comes from the Greek language, and in Greece we say, *emma,* which basically means blood. Haematology is the study of blood.'

I looked at my sister. 'Emma means blood?'

'In Greek,' my mother said.

'You named Emma after blood?'

My mother pressed the big green button that opened the doors. 'Grace,' she said, 'Please, don't start now.'

We didn't have to tell anyone who we were. People looked at us. They came. They said things like, 'Oh you're Emma. We've been expecting you.' It felt as though a concierge might take our bags, as though we were on holiday, but then the nurses were there, and the doctors too, and instead of hotel keys, the receptionist gave us a brand-new manila file with just a slip of paper clipped to the front—a blood report with the words 'blast cells A.L.L?' handwritten on the bottom. The lights were bright, and it was cold.

In the waiting area, while other families looked at us and then looked away, I settled firmly on the word haematology. I didn't want Emma to have cancer. I didn't think she needed a transplant. She already had all the care she wanted from my mother and me. Out of everything, haematology seemed like the lesser thing. Plus, she *was* 'Emma', and 'Emma' sounded like blood. My mother mustn't have realised this when she named her. It must've slipped her mind, and now we were here because of her carelessness, and, to me, that absolutely made sense.

Then Emma's doctor came. She was tall and tanned with long shiny hair and a stethoscope, which was draped around her neck. Instead of an overcoat, her clothes were flowery, pink and sweet. She said, 'Emma, hello.' Then she touched my mum on the arm and asked, 'What happened today?'

Mum said, 'I'm worried because no-one says much, and everyone prioritised her. The GP ordered these blood tests, but then the nurse at the clinic down south refused to do them. She said Emma was a child, and children need two nurses not one, and could I come back in the morning, but when I told her we lived out of town, she backed down and read the request. Then she took Emma in.'

Mum spoke of the bruises and the hay fever and the sore legs. She said, 'I thought I was paranoid taking her to the doctor. I thought she'd send me home, tell me not to worry. I thought she'd say I was silly and it was just growing pains.' Mum talked and talked and talked. She explained about the thing I saw in Emma's eye, the dots on her skin and the coughing. She didn't stop for I don't know how long. She spoke quickly and with little breath, and when I heard that crack in her voice, that break, everything that had frightened me began to take shape. She said, 'Personally I can't see anything wrong with her eye. I don't think her eye is the issue.'

I gripped my books, conscious I had nothing to stir, no wood to touch, no egg to make. The bags still pulled at my shoulders. Imaginary ants crawled in the space between my stomach and the elastic of my school skirt.

'It was a tiring day,' my mother continued. 'Not long after we returned home, I had a phone call. We packed our bags and drove all the way here.' She ended exactly where she began. 'I'm worried.'

Then the doctor spoke, 'Everyone prioritised her because they were worried too.'

I stood by the wall, leaned up against it. One minute we had our normal at-home lives and then the next we were being ushered through elevators and hallways from department to department. Emma had a chest x-ray while I lingered on the other side of a lead door. There was an ultrasound too, a radiologist's face, and the stress in my mother's voice: 'You don't see anything concerning, do you?' The whole time, the bags pulled at my shoulders and the elastic irritated me. Then we were back again. Or maybe we never left. Maybe these things came first. I can't remember. I won't remember. The bags cut into my skin. I stood by the wall. The doctor with the pretty hair and tanned skin started walking again. She took us deeper into that ward as though we were falling deeper into sleep.

'I must warn you,' she said. 'Things can be quite confronting in here.'

The children were pale, and they didn't have hair. Or if they did it was sparse and wispy in the same way steam rising from a pot of boiling water is wispy. There were IV poles, wheelchairs and blood pressure machines all down the corridor. There were Halloween decorations— orange pumpkins, skulls, black paper chains—all stuffed and poking out of packing boxes. Everyone seemed at once horrific and at home. There was a boy, maybe Emma's age, wheeling around on a ride-on tractor with the biggest smile on his face and a funny thin tube poking out from beneath his hospital shirt. There was one a few years older than me too, but somehow small. He wore a fluffy bathrobe over a pair of soft pyjamas. There was a drag in his foot. He smiled at me and he smiled at Emma. He told us that his name was David, and that everything would be okay. I didn't know it then, but David had a brother. David was like Emma, and his brother was like me.

You know what it felt like? It felt like Emma and I were on a school excursion. It felt like this wasn't really for us but rather something we were able to see. It felt like the time my class went to the pioneer house and the cheese factory. We were outside of that too, and were allowed to peer in, and then the school day ended, and we hopped on the bus and off we went home again. That's what it was—all of this—except this time there would be no bell, no bus ride, no follow up assignment, no dinnertime 'How was your trip, love?'

I put our bags in the corner of Emma's room. My shoulders hurt. The straps had cut into my skin. It was so white in that room, as white as Alice down the rabbit hole, and as disorientating too. Emma tried to wriggle her way onto the bed, but the bed was large, and she seemed so small. I grabbed her hand and helped her up. She kicked her shoes off. When they fell, they landed upside down, and the sparkles at the heel caught the light yet again. Mum paired these shoes neatly beneath the bed. She held Emma's feet, rubbed them, put socks on them. We weren't just Alice, we were Dorothy too. We were in a whirlwind *and* down a rabbit hole. We had walked through meadows and fallen into wide chasms that took us to places we had no idea existed. We were big. We were little. We didn't know what was happening, but we knew that there was no going home.

The doctor took a stethoscope to Emma's chest. She placed her fingers along either side of her neck and made her go, 'Ahhh.' Then she shone a torch into her ears, felt her tummy, 'Does it hurt when I press here?'

'Here?'

'Here?'

She whacked Emma's elbows and knees with a little hammer. Then she banged her wrist and her ankles too. She said, 'Emma, this is the strong girl test. I'm going to push your arms down, and your job is to stop me.

You can't let me win okay? Ready, steady, go ... stop me, stop me, stop me. Now the same with your legs. Go! Good girl.'

She scanned Emma top to bottom, stood her up, 'Can you walk an imaginary tightrope?'

'And now on tiptoes?'

'And on your heels?'

'Good,' she said. 'Good.' Then she grabbed her torch again. 'Let's cover your left eye. How many fingers am I holding up?'

'Two.'

'Now?'

'One.'

'Now?'

'Four.'

'And also your right. How many fingers?'

'Three.'

'Now?'

'Two.'

'Now?'

'One.'

'Good. Great,' she said. 'What I'm going to do now is shine the torch into your eyes. I want you to stare at the picture on the wall behind me. Try your hardest not to blink or shift your gaze, okay?'

'Okay,' Emma said, and then the doctor dimmed the lights and switched her torch back on. She shone that torch right into Emma's eyes. She looked at one eye and then the other. She said absolutely nothing, turned the light back on and walked out of the room.

My mother put her face in her hands.

I pulled at the collar of my school shirt. The skin beneath was as red as Emma's shoes, but the pain had all but gone. My fingers, my legs and my arms were numb. I looked at my hands. I could see them, move them, but they somehow felt detached. I opened *Heidi*, read a paragraph, reached the end of the page, but then I lost my place. The words circled around all the way to the beginning again.

The doctor returned. Then two nurses came. They bounced in with big smiles and bright ribbons in their hair. They spoke in fluids and milligrams and said things like, 'Come with me, princess,' and 'Oh what a beautiful child you are.' Emma put her hand in one of their hands and off she went, skipping with a renewed energy to wherever it was they took her. They whisked her through corridors. They whisked my mother too. They were storybook characters—these nurses—or colourful dancers in a children's television show.

In the meantime, the doctor scratched notes into Emma's file. I played with the bed's remote controls: lifted the bed up, pushed it down, tilted the top, made it flat. I sat on the edge and swung my legs over the side. I unzipped my bag and scrounged for a jumper.

'Are you okay?' the doctor said.

'Yes,' I replied. Then, 'No.' Then, 'I don't know.' Half my clothes were on the bed: undies, pyjamas, but not a jumper in sight.

The doctor left just as quickly as she came, but then she returned with a blanket. She wrapped it around my back and shoulders. 'Have this,' she said.

'Where did they take her?' I asked.

'Fluids,' she replied.

Then the dinner lady came carrying a tray. She said, 'Will your sister like something to eat?'

I shrugged, 'What is it?'

She lifted the lid to show me saucy beef pasta with steamed broccoli and crinkle cut carrots to the side. I looked at it and crinkled my nose myself. I knew my sister. If I couldn't stomach the meal, there was no way she would, so I shook my head and spoke with a confidence I didn't know I had. 'Do you think someone could organise Rice Bubbles instead?'

The orderly nodded. 'Yes of course,' she said.

Then the doctor said, 'Come with me,' and we too went around the corridors and rooms and tucked away tunnels until finally we stood in front of an open cupboard full of hand-stitched linen. The doctor said, 'How about you choose a quilt for your sister.' I stood in front of a cupboard full of colour, full of bright patterns—top to bottom, the whole cupboard. It was so weird that it couldn't have been anything other than a dream. Where else but a dream could you be in hospital, in front of a cupboard of quilted linen? And yet, there I was, and all I wanted was to do a good job. I wanted to please both the doctor and my sister. I wanted to pick the quilt Emma loved best.

The doctor left, and I stood there unsure where to begin. I pulled out all the pinks and reds and yellows, all the stripes, the flowers, and the sewn-on pictures of puppies and Barbie dolls. I lay them on the floor, unfolded and folded again: choosing, not choosing. Then I heard a scream from the adjoining room. It was long and loud—Emma, so clearly Emma—and it made me want to run to her. It made me want to rip her out and save her from whatever it was they were doing in there. I left the quilts and rushed to the door. I stood in the doorway and looked up and down that corridor. I didn't see Emma, but David, the boy in the bathrobe, was out again. He walked past, slowly, so slowly, pulling his IV pole as though it was some kind of robot box.

Two was a good number for Emma: either this one or that. Two was what I concentrated on. It seemed urgent, this blanket choosing. If I chose the one she wanted ... If I did my best job ... If she came out of that room and was happy with what I picked ... If I ... It would be okay. So, I went back and stood in front of that cupboard. I folded everything away except for a pink quilt sewn with ballerinas and black tulle, and a red one that was decorated with rectangles and large orange cats.

Then Emma was in the doorway, all smiles with a colouring book tucked under one arm and a bright pink bandage wrapped around the other. Out from the bandage poked one of those thin clear tubes. Attached to that tube was an IV robot pole. Emma waved the book at me. 'Look!' she said. 'Look at what I got!'

I said, 'I have a present for you too.'

She chose the cat blanket. She trailed it behind her while Mum pushed the robot pole, its wheels shifting this way and that, its tube tangling in little spirals and knots. She chose the Rice Bubbles too.

From then on everything was measured. The nurses came with their clipboards and their notepads. They wanted to know what Emma ate, and how much she drank. 'Cereal,' I said. 'A glass of milk. A packet of sultanas.' They took her temperature, her blood pressure. They wrote it down, wrote *everything* down. There was a pan for whenever Emma went to the toilet. Mum carried the pan and pushed the robot pole in the same way she once pushed a pram. The toilet was down the hall. They went in, and when they came out, the pan was full. Mum wrote Emma's name and the time on the pan. She draped a white paper towel over the top. Then the nurses came and went to work with sticks and scales. They measured what went in and what came out. It seemed important, this in-out thing. I watched Emma: every bite and every sip.

Mum sat by Emma's bedside. She stretched her legs in her seat, and folded and unfolded her arms. Then Dad came. Suddenly out of nowhere, he was looking at Mum and taking her out of the room and into the hallway. I could see them both through the nurse's window: Mum standing close with her eyes just about shut; Dad tall and all encompassing, kissing her forehead, wrapping her up and speaking in those hushed tones.

Emma was breathing so peacefully. Her chest rose and fell. This couldn't be, I thought. It couldn't. I felt a lump in my throat: that same ball of anxiety I had many times before.

Conversations happened at the end of Emma's bed. Words were thrown about: leukaemia, cancer. I picked up bits and pieces: bone marrow and aspirate and platelet transfusion. Suddenly numbers became wholly important. I learnt about haemoglobins and neutrophils. I wrote them down, charted them in the same way we charted graphs at school. I ticked checkboxes on a theatre questionnaire. *When was the patient's last meal? And her drink? And does she have any coughs or colds?* Doctors came, and an anaesthetist too. I learnt about optic nerves and lumbar punctures. I learnt about the blood-brain barrier, and the central nervous system.

In the end, Emma's eye was both fine and not fine. A lady came with a puppet and a silly show about the factory that had the blood recipe all wrong and the medicine that was going to set it right, and in the meantime, the doctor with the pretty hair said things like, 'The good news is there is no central nervous system involvement, no disease within the eye and no something-something-occlusion.' She spoke to my mother, and to my father. She said no-one was quite sure why Emma saw double—perhaps it was muscular, perhaps something for glasses or surgery later, but for the moment this was not the priority.

Emma coloured in and laughed, and the conversations went on. The nurses pricked Emma's fingertips and wrapped them in bandages. My parents huddled in hallways. My father kissed my mother's forehead. The doctors came around with more words, and then my mother fainted—collapsed right there in the corridor outside my sister's room, collapsed—and the nurse said, 'When was the last time YOU ate?'

Other people came. They said, 'My name is ...' and 'I'm from ...' and they brought with them hampers and toothbrushes and soft toys. They blew up balloons shaped like butterflies and flowers. They drew my sister's blood and left information leaflets. They said, as they walked in with countless medicines, 'Can you confirm that this is Emma?' and 'When is her birthdate?' They gave her stickers, and tied ribbons to the end of her hospital bed.

The first bag of fluid the IV robot fed my sister was clear.

The second was hidden inside a blue bag. It said: '*Handle with care. Cytotoxic.*' The nurse put it together while wearing a disposable gown and safety glasses. My mother folded her arms and looked away. I stood tall. I held Emma's hand.

In the spring, I was to be a good girl. I was to read my book and do my homework and in general just be quiet and keep out of the way.

Mum stayed with Emma, and Dad took me back home. He made bacon for breakfast and I finally learned the number of minutes to boil that egg. I dipped my toast into the yolk. It was yellow and salty but not as salty as the ham. Dad ate the fatty rind like a cat eats a lizard.

'Mum says bacon is not good for you.'

Dad raised an eyebrow. 'Your mum says a lot of things.'

The curtains were shut and there were toys all over the house—Emma's toys from before. Her canvas sneakers still had sand in them.

At school, I made necklaces out of daisy weeds. I plucked the petals and played, 'He loves me, he loves me not.' It didn't much matter that I was thirteen and growing. Spring made me feel small again. Spring was kiss-chasey and running and smooching, and everybody knew that the tepee was home. I watched all this from the wooden steps of our classroom transportable, and when Jason Everingham grabbed me from behind and I screamed and wiped his awful sloppy kiss away, he told me—quite calmly—that he was going to kiss me, that this would be his job, what he would do for the rest of his life. From then on, I hid in the tepee, or else I played along the edges of the oval where I picked cicadas out of the trees and held them in the hollow I made with my clasped palms.

Sometimes I went to the library. I looked up 'leukaemia' and read detailed encyclopaedia entries that could have easily been pocket-folded hospital leaflets. But when it came to stories, I barely read except to find comfort in the kind of books that started on page one and finished by ten or in the kind of myths whose plots I had already heard before.

The school was hot, the fans were whirring and the sprinklers were on all day. As we edged closer to the end of the school year, the rules relaxed. One Friday afternoon my friends and I found ourselves next to a long set of rusty wet pipes where we splashed and screamed and played as if there were no problems in any of our lives, no leukaemia, no upsets. We were not the blonde girls, nor the netball champions, but rather the girls whose mothers or fathers were born overseas, or else the Noongar girls, who told a different kind of Peel history to the one we had learnt at school. Beneath the water that rained out of those rusty pipes, we stretched our legs out, shared swear words and slang words and other words too. I taught the girls how to say, 'Hi' and, 'come on' and 'let's go' in Greek, and in return I learned that *kaya* meant 'hello' and *boorda* was what people said instead of 'see you soon'.

That same Friday, Dad picked me up before the bell and yelled at me for being sopping wet in class. He said, 'You little rat of a kid. You'll ruin my car seats, you know that?' and as we streamed past the bushland towards the city, I thought of the pink reflection on the river near the hospital, the clouds that were shaped like kangaroos and bunnies, and the milk arrowroots that my mother often kept in her handbag. It was hard to imagine Emma in hospital. Beyond the library, beyond what I found in medical definitions and pamphlets, I still wanted to think of her like me and the other girls, drenched and sharing stories with her friends. I wanted to think of her with my mother, both of them warm in the sunshine of the kind of childhood that Emma never actually had.

13

In the beginning, Emma and my mother all but lived on those hospital grounds. If it wasn't the cancer, it was a soaring temperature, bad blood counts, bacteria and even migraines which came from the medicines she was taking. Chemotherapy shut her immune system down and made her susceptible to all sorts of other illness. All the things we previously took for granted—a little dirt in the park, leftovers, swimming pools, crowds and even the lake—now threatened to harm her. There were rules, radiuses she had to abide by, distances that imprisoned both her and my mother. In the whole of Western Australia, there was only one place to treat a child with cancer, and now having crossed the threshold into that place, Emma and my mother were no longer allowed to come home. Home was too far, too many kilometres, too risky. Instead, Emma had a room and an IV robot on the ward for whenever she was sick, and a charity apartment across the road for the times when she was well. It was small, this apartment, a tiny bedsit with just one place to sleep, a bathroom and a communal living hall, but so long as Emma needed her treatment and a doctor nearby, home was a mythical creature replaced instead with a frightening wave of hospital and hostel. In and out my sister and mother went—pendulums from the ward to their halfway house.

I would've liked to have been a pendulum too. It would've been nice to say that Dad and I were country and city and all the road in-between, that our bags were always packed and always ready, and that we visited from time to time, but as it was, Dad and I left Emma and my mother to themselves. We visited once or twice while Emma was an inpatient, but not when she was well enough to leave the ward.

November passed, and December came. Without Emma, I went to sleep always somehow touching the wooden headboard behind me. I stirred the chocolate dots out of my Milo, raced against the microwave clock, held my breath whenever Dad drove past the cemetery, counted stairs, and said, as if up into the stars and across the sky, 'sweet dreams, see you soon' while adding a silent 'alive' in my head. Sleep claimed me easily. Sleep felt like waking from the nightmare. I rested heavily, deeply and darkly. I did not dream. Sleep was vast and black and protective. I yearned for it, fell into it. In sleep, things seemed to correct themselves. Although there were no pictures, Emma was Emma, Mum was Mum, and Dad was Dad. But then, when eventually my dreams did return, they seemed more real than real. Sometimes it was as though I was pressed on my bed, weighed down with a hand that was heavy and scorched with fire. Other times it was as though Emma was there, a version of her. She was beside me or on me, breathing against my neck or my cheek. I'd think, 'Emma, is that you? Is that really you?' and then I'd hear a boom in my ear, a resounding yes that reverberated down my spine and rammed me across the bed. Always I woke with a twisted sensation to my chest.

In the meantime, Dad had his friends over. They drank. They smoked. They carried on about that boss of theirs, the greenies and the government cuts. 'How's that little girl of yours?' one of them asked one late afternoon.

Dad said, 'Yeah, she made remission the other day.'

The boys cheered—all of them. They patted Dad on the back.

My ears pricked up. 'Is she coming home?' I asked.

Dad shook his head, stood and walked to the esky in the corner of our patio. As he grabbed himself another beer, he said. 'Love, that cancer's a prick of a thing. It'll come back if they give up too soon.'

'What do you mean?'

'I mean, Emma and your mother are staying a few months more.'

'Until when?'

'Don't know. A few months.'

One of Dad's friends spoke then. 'Reckon you and your missus will stick together now?'

Dad replied, 'If she'll have me back, I won't turn her down,' and everyone laughed. Everyone, except for me.

I grew accustomed to my lonely summer. I tidied Emma's room, tipped the sand out of her shoes and into the garden, and remembered my birthday at the lake and how it was Harriet who returned those shoes to us. How she got chatting with my mother. How they both seemed so excited to have nearly the same geographical coordinates running through their veins. I played on the trampoline and thought of Harriet precisely because I could not think of my mum. Mum was too far away, too occupied, but Harriet was surely somewhere near, also sharing those coordinates with me.

I wore bathers and ran under sprinklers. I snuck off to the lake, but then, when Harriet and Samuel were not there, I came home. In the kitchen, I hauled out the phonebook and flicked through page after page of tiny typeset, looking for every coupling of H and S that I could find. One, two, three, fifty phone numbers later, and I gave up again.

Outside, at the letterbox, I collected the mail, brought it all in and laid it on the counter. On the back page of our local paper, I saw an advert for a new marketplace coming soon—crafts and foods and all sorts of things. I saw an address too—around the corner, down the road, midway between our house and the lake. Sometimes, secretly, I walked past that same address and caught glimpses of Harriet watering the roses that lined the veranda, her back always somehow facing away from the street. Other times, I saw the shapes of Harriet and Samuel moving around at the side of the house, potting little olive trees and tending to them as if these trees were children themselves. In front of me, as they were, I no longer knew what to say. I didn't know how to reveal myself, how to put my hand up and ask for help. Something clamped inside of me and my voice shut down.

At home, I sat cross-legged in front of our drawer full of family photos. In that drawer, I flicked through my parents' wedding album and pored over pictures of my parents standing before an elaborately dressed Orthodox priest. They drank church wine together. They exchanged rings together. They wore white crowns joined with string. Dad held my mother's hand. After the wedding, there was a cottage home, pizza on a balmy night, movies at the drive-ins, fish and chips and lazy evenings along the coast. There were holiday snaps and landscape postcards, my mother in sarongs and bikinis, Asian paradises, Mediterranean beaches, my grandmother's village, an olive farm, my great-grandparents—strangers to me—standing on either side of a donkey, and my dad: noticeably fair and freckled and out of place. Then my mother's belly ballooned, and the holiday snaps slowed down. Dad leaned against a faded 'For Sale' sign with a goofy smile and a set of dangling house keys. Big dreams were written all over his face, like 'this is it, this is what it's all about.' We were leaving—me included now—arriving at this lake town. Dad and I splashed in the shallow but choppy waters of Preston Beach —the beach of our Boxing Days, long weekends and 'it's hot out, who wants to go for a swim?' I wore a green bathing suit trimmed with dotted frills, and Dad held me with my arms wrapped firmly around his shoulders and neck. Mum was there too, on the beach, a high angle camera shot, the glint of light in her sunnies and her hand shielding her eyes.

Then, in other photos, along came Emma. Emma was a baby, pink and little, a series of close-up fingers and lips, a sock-covered foot. The beach pictures seemed to come to a halt. If there were any at all, they were of Dad with his mates, the images set against a darkening light, an esky between bait buckets and fishing rods wedged deep in the sand. Emma grew older and took a few wobbly steps on her feet. She wore her best clothes, and she held onto the backyard clothesline with a big smile on her face and a 'watch what I can do' gape to her mouth. She looked at the camera—at my mother. Her cheeks were fat and pink. Her lips had the shine of saliva. Her eyes were how eyes ought to have been; they were bright and wide and full of life. In the meantime, I was dressed in my 'at-home' clothes, barefooted and grubby in cotton shorts and a too-small top. Behind that camera my mother cooed at Emma and simultaneously chided me. 'Why don't you wear your nice skirt? Smile Grace, for the love of God, smile.' I managed—it seemed—something rather gritted. When the camera clicked, I was captured—in the same way criminals are captured on closed circuit television, giving Emma what my mother claimed was 'the evil eye'.

Photos and memories eventually blended into each other, and it wasn't long before I began blaming myself for the cancer. I remembered all the times I was angry with Emma, the times I told her that I'd wish she'd never been born, and even the times we made up tennis games like 'Ghosts', for example, and the sound of my satisfied voice each time she missed the ball: 'You're sick, Emma ... you're buried ... you're a skeleton ... you're a ghost.'

Then, on one of those photo-looking days, the phone rang. It rang in the background, and Dad picked up and all I could hear was his muffled voice. In my hand, Emma was on her tricycle, ice-cream on her face and hair stuck to her cheeks. Emma was fixed in time, wearing thick-ribboned piggy-tails, and holding on to that yellow bear of hers. Emma was pretty and photogenic.

◉ ◉ ◉

In the car, on the way to the city, I was scared, but I didn't know what I was scared of. I was trying to remember something, though I wasn't sure what I had forgotten. When we reached the hospital, Dad and I walked through those same halls, in that same fluorescent stillness, during those same familiar hours as my mother, Emma and I once had. I think a part of me expected ... I don't know what I expected. Neither Mum nor Emma looked anything like their former selves. Gone were most of my sister's curls. Gone was her fleshy padding. She was elfin, skinner than ever before. Mum too had lost weight. While I wore the healthy tan of summer—all tank tops and colours—Mum and Emma looked as though they had just clawed their way out of ice.

At first, Dad made an impressive effort. He stayed overnight with Emma, told my mother to take a break, have a rest, a good sleep. He made friends with the nurses and the doctors. He bought popcorn, ice-cream and bread for the ward. Pikelets and muffins and trays of sausage rolls appeared as if out of nowhere. When Emma pushed her fruit away, Dad did not yell like he had often yelled at home, but rather he cleared her plate and rearranged Emma's otherwise discarded watermelon and blueberries into elaborate cartoon shapes. He made elephants and spiders and boats with mango hulls and cantaloupe sails. While my mother wrung a paper napkin as though it were a rope, Dad's accolades circled in rings of applause.

'How lovely!'

'How lucky!'

'What a wonderful dad you have!'

But then familiar cracks began to show. Dad kept his shoes on and traipsed dirt through the ward. He stood on the end of Emma's bed to change the channel on the television and left the imprint of his soles on her sheets. My mother stripped those sheets quickly and quietly. She found clean linen in the storage room and new blankets too. She washed the cat-quilt in the parent laundry, remade the bed and said, not straight away but soon after, 'Actually, I'd like it if you took your shoes off.' Then she gave Dad the anti-bacterial gel and asked him to wash his hands. She said, 'Emma has no immunity. She can't cope with dirt. I saw one of the oncologists at the main entrance the other day. He was wiping his shoes on the mat, really giving them a good scrub.'

Dad said, 'But that's alright.'

And when Mum replied, 'Why would you say that? I don't understand what you're trying to say,' Dad dismissed her with a quick, 'It is what it is.'

'What does that even mean?' Mum asked.

He said, 'You can either be happy or sad about her being here. You can overreact or be calm. Either way, she is here, and she has cancer, and nothing I do or don't do is going to change that fact. It's a question of attitude.'

'I don't get you,' my mother said. But she did, really. She got him loud and clear. My parents, they would always be oppositional, always conflicting. That was the way it would always be.

Dad took his shoes off and stunk out Emma's room.

My mother asked him to wash his feet.

Dad said, 'I don't care about my feet. I don't care. I don't care. I don't care.'

'That's the problem,' my mother snapped.

'I DON'T CARE. I DON'T CARE. I DON'T CARE,' he said, stomping around.

Emma held onto her yellow bear and climbed onto our mother's lap, the IV tubes tangling around her leg. I grabbed the gel, pumped a gentle drop onto my palm, and while the smell seeped into my flesh, I said as petulantly as I could, 'I'm bored. I'm tired.' Emma's illness was predictable. It followed a set pattern, a protocol which laid out all the possibilities, good and bad. Even if we weren't sure what was happening, a doctor or a nurse was. Dad, however, was not predictable. 'I'm bored,' I said again, mostly to shift the tension. 'This is so unfair.'

Mum looked at me. 'If you're so put out, why don't you take your dad and go home.'

Emma said, 'Daddy, poooooh, your feet are smelly.'

And Dad replied with a cold, 'You never noticed until your mother started carrying on.'

Emma paused, put on a mature grown-up voice. 'Daddy, please clean your feet.'

On the day I held my mother tight and begged her to let me stay, Dad went on a shopping spree. He bought a kayak, and then another, and when my mother questioned him for spending so much money, he told her to deal with things her way and leave him to deal with them as he saw fit. He bought roof-racks, safety jackets, water shoes, oars. He bought straps to hold the kayaks in place, a wetsuit, a paddle leash, a backrest, three vests, a pair of board-shorts, a fishing rod, hooks, a bucket and a spare line. He went to the electronics store and bought a dozen movies and a portable DVD player to watch those movies on. He put the movies on Emma's bed. He filled Emma up full of toys and crowded her room. He bought a gigantic teddy bear, three large 'Get Well' balloons and a set of pink flower hairclips. My mother whisked these clips away as swiftly as the orderlies whisked Emma's fallen strands from the floor. She sat with Emma, kissed her thinning crown, her widening part and the wispy bits around her face that still held strong.

In all of this, a coordinating nurse came to talk to my mother about bone marrow registries and the urgency of finding a donor match for Emma should she ever need a transplant. The nurse was careful with her words, slow, different to the round of information we had all received when Emma was first diagnosed. Instead, the nurse used words like 'precautionary'. She gave statistics. She said it was a simple blood test and told us there was a one in four chance the best match would be me. Mum signed the forms, and off I went, out to another room where I sat on a large and rigid chair and stretched my arm for a phlebotomist to bleed.

That same afternoon, Santa came by with his bag bulging full of presents. Emma opened them all, creased and crinkled paper falling everywhere while a crowd of children grew in the doorway. My mother posed for a picture with both Emma and Santa. Santa had make-believe glasses and cotton-balls glued to his eyebrows. Emma held a bumblebee made of red and black balloons. She wore bright pink leggings, a green button-up hospital shirt. Her eyes were dark circles, her hair extraordinarily sparse, her eyebrows patchy, her face washed with a pale, colourless glow. She rested her head against my mother's chest. There were sutures on her neck, and a clear dressing—a visual and public reminder of the related sutures that sat beneath her armpit, the ones that covered the bump no-one was allowed to touch, the bump that hurt her and hurt her until finally it became a part of her, beneath her skin, this bump that stopped her from sleeping on her side, this valve that took the medicines her veins were too fragile for—her port.

Then someone snapped a camera. My mother smiled directly at it: this wide over-compensating, unreal smile. Her face was full of wrinkles. She wore no make-up. Her hair was pulled into a severe yet hand-brushed bun. I looked down at the dressing on the crease of my elbow, a counterpoint for the dressings Emma had. Then I looked up again. It was brutal, the pain on my mother's face. It powered through that Christmas smile of hers and told its own truth.

14

At home, the kayaks sprawled in opposite diagonals across our living room and into the kitchen where they formed a dangerous and unstable crisscross that I stepped on and rode like a surfboard whenever I needed so much as a drink of water. Dad dumped the wetsuits, vests and shoes on top of our couch. He discarded the fluffy bear near the television, and the Santa costume in the corner where the Christmas tree ought to have been. Mail piled up along our breakfast bar. Community newspapers and advertising pamphlets littered our coffee and kitchen tables. Plastic grocery bags bursting with empty packets of cereal, clinking beer bottles and old styrofoam trays began to fill all our remaining spaces.

Dad was a spinning top. Either he shouted, or he clung. If he lay on the couch, he wanted me nearby on the floor. If he watched TV, he called and sought me out. 'Where are you?' he said. 'What are you doing? Come see this.' He was high excitement mixed with the kind of irritability that made me take flight firstly to the end of Harriet's street where I remained too afraid—or too shy maybe—to announce myself, and then secondly to the familiar drapes and dapples of leaves that opened into the lake.

Beneath that hidden shade, I tried my best to read. I wanted to calm the words in even my simplest books. I wanted to see them just once on the page without having them circle around, but when that failed to happen, I let myself slip back into the stories my mother once told Emma and me. I remembered Persephone picking flowers in the meadow, and Hades abducting her into the opulent walls and halls of his Underworld. I remembered Demeter calling from above, searching for her daughter, shouting 'Kore! Kore!! Kore!!!' until she was shrill with so much grief that all the flowers and crops withered and died. I remembered Zeus—the way he sent his son down to bargain for Persephone's life, and Demeter descending those steps, and Hades—cunning Hades—tricking Persephone into eating six pomegranate seeds so as to bind her to him. And then finally, I remembered the storm that came when the all-powerful, all-masculine Zeus ordered them all to accept that Persephone would divide her time between mother and abductor. But what came most strongly to me, when the words of my books refused to stay still against my eyes, were the additions my mother made and the connections she found between hardship and knowledge—*káto* and katabasis and *katálava*—and I wondered if this was the same in English with the words 'under' and 'Underworld' and 'understood', and if it was what my mother had been trying to teach us all along.

I sat on the edge of that lake beneath my tree. Instead of reading, I began to dig at the ground with a stick. The thrombolites were exposed and encrusted with salt once more. Here and there, tree-trunks were black with disease, but all the same, that shoreline suddenly made sense to me. It was 'beneath', 'under', 'down', but also, it was visible now, on the surface. It was what people wouldn't normally see.

Dad hated me going to the lake. He had to know exactly where I was. He had to pinpoint me. The more I ran off, the more he reined me in. The more he reined me, the more I left.

'Can I go to ...' I asked. 'Can I sleep at ...' 'Can I hang out with ...'

'No,' Dad said. No and no and no.

I dug my heels in. 'I'm thirteen,' I shouted. 'You can't control me. You can't tell me what to do. You don't know anything about me.'

'I don't need to Grace,' he said. 'What I know is boys. I used to be one. I know what they're thinking when they look at you.'

'Shut up,' I said.

'Don't you tell me to shut up.'

'SHUT UP,' I said again.

On the Monday before Christmas, instead of going to work, Dad slept on the floor in front of our television. His stomach moved up and down to the rhythm of his breath, and he did not wake, not until late afternoon. In the evening, still unwashed and unshaven, he stood on the receiving end of our phone and said his calmest, most professional voice, 'Oh I see. Okay. No worries,' but when he hung up, he looked at me and laughed—he laughed—and then he said, 'Bullshit those cheap pricks saying not enough work.'

'What happened?' I asked, because I felt like I needed to ask something.

'Laid me off, that's what. Your sister's in hospital and they ring just before Christmas and ...' He kept going and going, grabbing a can of beer and opening the tab. He drank it, all the time pacing from the kitchen to the television to outside and back again.

I scrounged the fridge for something to make for dinner. I put slices of cucumber on a plate and carrot sticks too. I boiled eggs, grated cheese and made toast for the both of us. I dolloped yoghurt into a small bowl. When Dad sat down to dinner, he said, 'Ah love, you're a good kid.' And then he said, 'Maybe it's for the best, hey. Spend a bit of time with you.'

The very next day he took me fishing. He strung one of the kayaks to his roof-racks. As we drove in the exact opposite direction from Mum and Emma, south towards Preston Beach, he chirped about the fish we would catch and the prospect of rowing out to sea. But when we reached the beach, he said it looked dangerous out, and then he told me to leave the kayak on top of the car. The path from the car park down to the beach was flat and hard. The sea was bright, blue and soft. It wasn't rough. It wasn't scary. I would've helped carry the boat.

But Dad said, 'No,' in that way of his.

Instead of paddling, I watched him cast a single line from the shore. I hung back near the dunes and scratched pictures in the sand. He had promised the boat, but then he had backed out. I called to him, 'I always do what *you* want to do. I always listen to what *you* say.' I begged, 'Please Dad, can't we take the kayak out?'

Dad reeled in and reeled out. He said, 'It's not safe.' His face was steely, and then it changed yet again. He caught a fish—just one—and even though it was obviously too small to keep, he turned to me and celebrated by dancing like a dangly puppet on a string, like one of those clown things. I knew, instinctively, that my job was to laugh. So long as Dad was happy, so long as my eyes were directed at him, so long as it was me in front of him and not Emma, everything was alright. Emma needed Mum, and Dad needed me.

Christmas Day came. Dad didn't shave, we didn't go to church and there was no special lunch. Instead of travelling to see Emma and Mum, we drove once more in the direction of the sea. Dad had his esky and the fishing lines. The ocean was even calmer, but the kayak remained strung just as it did the day before. Dad caught another fish—a full-sized one this time—and so he danced all over again. He cracked a beer, and then another. He sat back with his rod and the spent bottles wedged in the sand.

For a long time, I played nearby. Just to the north of us was a groyne that had been made out of a series of car tyres. I went to the groyne and skipped up and down the top of it in the same way I might have had I been playing hopscotch. Then I sat down just like my dad had, but instead of the beach, I sat on one of the tyres. It was warm and dusty against my skin, but it still somehow comforted me. The water was lapping up ahead but it did not quite reach the tyre I was sitting on. I imagined my mother with me and Emma, all of us, making sandcastles complete with moats and drawbridges. I imagined Dad fishing up ahead, but Mum right with us, checking for sunscreen, offering juice, watching us go back and forth from the shore to fill our buckets with water. At one point, I glanced up towards the dunes and the car park. The kayak looked shiny on top of Dad's roof-racks. The sea looked calm. Dad had his hat over his face. His skin was tinged pink in the sun. The fishing line was slack, and then it yanked taut. He didn't at all try to reel in. 'Dad,' I called, but just as I thought, he had fallen asleep.

Before long I was at the car, untying those ropes and climbing along the driver's side doors. I touched the kayak, bobbed it back and forth, gently, not so gently, a little aggressively—push, pull, push, pull—rocking and rocking in bursts until it began to topple. Then I readied myself to catch it as it fell. I was going to catch that whole kayak—that's what I was thinking—I was going to catch it as it fell. But then the bitumen burned at my feet, I lost my balance, and the whole lot came crashing down.

Something cracked. One of the oars was wedged firmly beneath the hull. It was as crooked as an elbow that had bent the wrong way. The fibreglass was cracked too, chipped and scratched and full of marks on its smooth, shiny, never-wet surface.

◎ ◎ ◎

In the evening, Dad cleaned his gear under the tap out the front of our house. He slit, gutted and scaled the fish on a mat of newspapers. I circled him, stayed at his feet. Our carport stunk. The kayak was tied to the roof-racks. As Dad wrapped the cleaned fish in a spare sheet of paper, I said, 'Shall I help you lower the boat?'

'No,' he said. Then he reached out with the wrapped fish package. 'Take this inside, will you?'

'Gross! No!'

'Grace, if you don't take this after what happened, I'm likely to lose my temper.'

'No!' I said again.

Dad picked up a scrap of something that had once come from inside the fish. It was squashy and smelly and grey. It slid through his fingers. He said, 'If you don't do as I say, I'm going to wipe you full of guts.'

'Dad,' I said.

'Now!' he insisted. Then he lunged forward with the fish guts.

I screamed and ran to Emma's room where I slammed the door and sat on the edge of her bed. On her table, just beneath the lampshade, was a small half-eaten packet of sultanas. The lid was open, and the sultanas were hard and crystallised to touch. I grabbed one nonetheless, rolled it tentatively in my mouth and then squashed it between my teeth. It was stale and gross, but not as gross as the fish. I grabbed another and then another, and then I lay back on Emma's bed and wrapped my arms around the little pink lamb she kept on her pillow. I cuddled him close. He wasn't Yellow Bear, but he still smelled like the soap Emma used at night, her toothpaste and the faint wash of her shampoo.

Dad found me then. He wasn't carrying the guts, but his hands still had a slippery sheen. 'Come help with the barbie,' he said. It was afternoon, neither lunch nor dinner. I was hungry. I would've eaten almost anything, even that fish if he hadn't made such a show about it. It was Christmas, but it wasn't how Christmas normally went.

I held Lamb tightly. 'GET,' I said, strongly and sharply like the boys at school did whenever they fought with one another.

'Grace. Don't talk to me that way.'

'GET!!' I yelled, standing up again.

'GET!' I repeated as I shoved past him and out of my sister's bedroom. As Dad surged forward, I ducked and weaved and ran my way outside.

Then Dad shut the back door and locked me out.

I held Lamb. I held the sultanas too. I wasn't wearing shoes. My hair was matted and damp, still salty from the morning.

I wanted so much to go to the lake. I wanted to find Harriet, to go past the house she shared with Samuel and eat for Christmas all the things—honeyed walnuts and icing-sugar almond cookies—that my mother might have made. I wanted Harriet to *be* my mother, if for a moment, just so I could have a mother near me again, but I knew that if I did go to the lake and she wasn't there, or if I found myself at her front porch and failed to summon the courage to knock on the door, or worse, if I did knock only to be ushered away, then I wouldn't know what to do next.

So instead, I climbed onto the trampoline, and I jumped for a long time, just jumping and jumping, as if I was in slow motion, as if my little sister was there bouncing with me. Then, when I tired of this, I climbed back down and went to the garden shed. At the very top of one of the shelves, tucked behind a toolbox and a tangled pile of electrical cords, was Dad's half-finished packet of cigarettes, the same cigarettes that he pulled out whenever he had friends over. Inside that packet, in amongst folded, crisp foil, there were exactly twelve perfectly rolled paper sticks. They smelt sweet. Their stubs were yellow. I pulled one out and held it between my index and ring fingers.

Near the cords was a little gas lighter, left there, I suppose, by my dad. I grabbed the lighter and pulled down at the ignition wheel. As soon as the flame burnt into the cigarette, the sweetness vanished, and the tobacco lit into something repelling and bitter. It shocked me, this bitterness. It felt dry on my tongue and charred. In that shed, crouched in a dark corner, with my legs tucked right to my buttocks and Lamb by my feet, I smoked because I had to. I wasn't doing it to be cool, or to stay warm, or to fit in with anyone from school; I was smoking to get cancer. 'I wish I had cancer,' I said aloud, as if to God, or to the universe, or to whoever it was in the Underworld that heard those things and made them happen. 'I wish it was me. Not her. Me.'

When I finished, I put the stub out along the concrete. I smoked another, and then one more. I littered the floor full of yellow cigarette butts. I left them there—all of them—and as I stood up again, I imagined my mother coming home, cleaning up, seeing them scuffed and scattered, and hearing—knowing—the words I could not say. It comforted me just to think about it. 'I'm thirsty, Mum. I'm hungry. It's warm outside, but I'm actually cold.'

Then the phone rang. I heard it even from where I stood. Dad picked it up and although his voice was muffled and brief, I knew without asking who it was on the other end. He did not come to find me. He did not call my name. Just as quickly as he first answered the phone, he hung it up. The sliding door to our patio opened and shut. Dad shuffled around the barbecue. I could smell dinner: a mismatching of fish grilled with sausages and onions that he had caramelised into a big wet pile. The phone rang again, but this time Dad let it ring out. It came at me, drifting through that sliding door.

I washed my face at the tap out the back. I washed my mouth too. I drank and drank and drank and tried my hardest to wet the smoky burn I felt within my cheeks. The water spilled down my chin, onto the paving bricks, and then onto the grass where it bounced on a dirty patch and splashed against my feet. In that splash, I found a beetle. He was small and round. I picked him up with the scoop of my hand. He was black and shiny, and his barbed legs felt ticklish on my skin. He was mine, and I held him, and I rotated my palm, up and flat, up and flat, in half-formed arcs, so that no matter what he did he could not get away. I held Lamb in one hand and the beetle in the other, and in that moment, I felt it again: I was thirteen and a grown up, but also, I was young enough to want Lamb not for Emma but back to me.

Then Dad shouted, 'Barbie's ready,' about the same time as the phone rang again. I brushed the beetle back onto the earth and sped through the garden, past my father, through the patio door, ripping the door open, picking the phone up only just in time.

It was my mother. 'Oh, I was about to give up,' she said.

'Merry Christmas, Mum.'

'Have you had a lovely day?'

'Yes,' I lied, and then I told her that Dad sang carols, and we had presents, and he took me to lunch. I said, 'We went to the vineyard actually. There were lots of people, not just Dad and me.'

And she said, 'Good, that's good,' with this breathlessness that made me feel my lying was exactly the right thing. She said, 'Oh that's wonderful. I'm so pleased to hear it.'

She told me that she and Emma had lunch with all the other families who couldn't go home, that they had a big roast and presents, and that the volunteers had come on Christmas Eve like elves to dress the tables with tinsel and ribbon-rimmed candles. There was so much food, she said. There were potatoes and salads and even a sticky-date pudding for dessert.

I said, 'Did Emma eat?'

'Actually yes,' my mother replied. 'She did.'

'Can I talk to her?'

'Of course,' Mum said, but when Emma took the phone, she didn't say a word. Mum giggled as Emma handed the receiver back. 'She's still a bit young. She's feeling shy on the phone. We walked, you know, after lunch. We went all the way around the block, maybe a kilometre or so. She managed it. Really, she did.'

I said, 'When are you coming home?'

And Mum replied, 'Honey, maybe around June or July. Middle of winter.'

I looked down to my lap, and then up again. I bit my lip and squeezed Lamb up into a one-armed hug.

Mum said, 'I have to go,' and 'Sweetheart, I love you,' at about the same time as I turned towards the patio door. Dad was on the other side, shutting the screen I had left open. His mouth was stretched over sausage and sliced bread. Sauce dripped down the sides.

DESCENT

15

Some people lie awake in the middle of the night because money troubles them. Others because they hate their jobs or because unhappiness plagues the way they move and shift in their everyday lives. In the houses next door and next door again, Rosa and Katerina likely lay awake remembering their long-gone husbands, the countries and families they once left behind, and even their black-sheep grandchildren who now fell into wrong crowds and found themselves mixed up in drink and drugs. In the house further along, the woman there perhaps wondered whether the hose was turned off or quietly flooding the garden. Maybe she thought of the illness that was slowly watering a hole in her husband's memory, or else of what this hole would soon mean. At Cole's, there were university exams to worry about, a separation of sorts and a boy who needed something more than just a warm meal and a place to kick his football.

It had been early when I arrived at work that morning. It had been early, and all the toys and activities were still packed away. Zoe had needed blood. Catherine had left but not really left. She had taken a walk to clear her head, and Simon was there, shoes on the bed, watching movies and hanging out with that little girl of his. They seemed to be having a good time. They were taking selfies, laughing and posting pictures online. Zoe's energy had picked up, and I was finishing my shift, handing her file over from Same Day Care to the inpatients section of our ward. Zoe had needed blood and insulin. She had a temperature, low to mid-grade. It was important that we pulled her sugars under control.

And then it was Simon who came out looking for a vomit bowl, who said, 'She's vomiting blood. It's black. It's blood.'

It had been early, and then it was well past my shift's end time. At the beach, the seagull's leg was bent in a knotty sling. Nate was there, and Alison too—their oversized beach bag spilling with oversized family things.

At night, every noise seemed so magnified: the fridge, a neighbour's air-conditioner running unnecessarily, the sound of the hot water storage system filling up, readying for the morning. Vibrations rang in my ears. I heard a plane overhead and a helicopter too, but it wasn't the sharp noises, it was the persistent ones—the drones—that stopped me from sleeping.

It was Halloween and then it was November. It was the day a pathologist wrote the words, 'blast cells A.L.L.?' on my sister's blood report.

Sometimes it was the haunting call of a bird that kept me awake.

It was a tiny pinprick mark on one of Zoe's calves, innocuous-looking, the kind of thing you don't quite register at the time but remember in retrospect. It was a tiny pinprick mark that blackened and grew.

16

Barely six in the morning, and already William was bouncing his ball and taking his marks as if he was directly beneath my window instead of across the road. Every now and then Cole called to him, 'William, breakfast!' or, 'William, you'll wake the neighbours!' or, 'William, come inside!!!' and intermittently, as William did as he was asked, the bouncing stopped, picked up, and then stopped again before fading in a way that suggested Cole had finally taken him down the street and to the park. Sunshine filtered through the blinds. I kicked the quilt off, and then the sheets, and then, finally after I relented to the growing heat, I made my way into the kitchen where I found the previous night's painting leaning up against the pantry door. In the fresh light of morning, it seemed amateurish and derivative. It was shiny and gold—not a drawing or an image but rather, hurried, unaccomplished brushstrokes. Long ago, I used to enjoy painting. I used to mix colours in this whimsical abstract style, and I used to draw bright storybook figures, which I then posted to Emma, and which, in the back and forth of our letter writing, kept us close even as we were towns and cities apart. Back then, if someone had asked what I wanted to be when I grew up, I might have said a painter, a teacher, a dancer, an artist, but now, looking at my underdeveloped painting skills, the thought occurred to me that I should just be grateful I became a nurse.

I switched the kettle on and crossed from the pantry to the fridge and then to the cupboard where I kept the cereal bowls and Harriet's old teacup. It was plain, this teacup—white bone china with scalloped spirals along the sides, a base that fanned a little and a handle that curled like a question mark. This one object in a collection of small objects that reminded me of her. I poured water into that cup and over a teabag. Then I squeezed the teabag with a spoon and made my breakfast. The previous day had been such a mess. Don't look back: that's what my mother and Harriet both often said. It was what I had somewhat internalised. 'Don't look back... Don't turn ... Keep going ...' No matter what the circumstances, I always pushed forward. I became a nurse, bought a house and slept with a married man. I went to the doctor and wrote a phone number on the top of a piece of paper, and then another phone number on the underside. Heads, I keep the baby; tails, I don't. But where was the thought in that? I just swum along. I floated on a splintered board and held on. What though if looking back was what I should have done? What if that pinprick mark on Zoe's skin was as recognisable as it ought to have been? Why not look back? Why not recover the steps I once took?

I reached for my phone, typed 'Yalgorup' into the search engine of my internet browser, and then 'Lake Clifton'. I changed the view on my Map App to 'Satellite' just to see the trees and rooftops and waterways of the place I used to call home. Then, right as I felt either a pang of morning sickness or a misplaced homesickness or sickness over what had happened at work, the phone rang.

'Grace, can you work a shift on Inpatients today?'

'No,' I wanted to say. Was it not my fault yesterday? 'How is Zoe?' I asked, not answering one way or the other.

'Stable,' Sarah, the nurse coordinator said. 'You did well,' she added. 'You were great.'

I swirled the last cooled remnants of my tea around the bottom of my cup.

'Can you come in?' Sarah repeated.

'I guess so,' I said, because work calling and me saying 'yes,' was now so routine that I rarely stopped to consider what it was I was feeling. Autopilot switched on. I took my dishes to the sink, brushed my teeth, showered, dressed, and made my bed, but then, just as I went back to the bathroom to fix my hair, I happened to glance at the small corked bottle of salt that I always kept on a shelf next to the mirror.

I had taken those salts from Harriet in the same way as I had also taken the teacup and an old set of Samuel's binoculars. I had carried them from home to home, wrapping them carefully into an ever-changing box of my 'most wanted things' until, one day, my mother, who was helping me settle into this final house, had come to me, bottle in hand. 'What do you want with this?' she asked, as if the very bottle held within it a substance best discarded.

At first I didn't quite know what to say. Inside that bottle was the memory of what I had done to Emma and what had happened at the lake that one awful day, but also inside it was my childhood, Emma following me, the two of us on the logs, exploring up and down the jetty there, looking at clouds. Inside was Harriet too, the things she taught me and also the things I knew. Most of all, though, if I were honest, was the sense that I could never throw this bottle away. Holding on to it was like dissolving dots in my Milo. 'I guess they make me think of those days back with Harriet and Samuel,' I half-said.

Mum looked at me and then looked away. Without returning her gaze, she said, 'I cannot understand why you would want to go back to that time.'

'It's not that time but that place,' I said. Then, as I took the bottle from her hands, and put it onto my bathroom shelf, I added, 'If I so want to, I can take a bath in that water and be right there all over again.'

Mum raised an eyebrow in that way of hers. '*If* you want to,' she said.

True to her word, the bottle had been on the same shelf so long that dust had collected on the top. I had never opened it, never smelled the salt inside, never dissolved that salt into a bath, never once wanted to look back as closely as I said I did, but now, as I finished pinning my hair and finished packing away my leftover clips and hair ties, the urge to run a bath grew. A familiar 'don't want to go to work' returned louder and with more insistence. My handbag was packed and my shoes were in my hand when I finally garnered the courage to ring the ward. 'Sarah, I'm not feeling well.' It wasn't a lie; I was tired, my back seemed tight, my stomach ached and there was a cramping sensation across my abdomen, like a stitch after running.

Sarah said, 'Oh okay. Please don't worry. Get the rest you need, and I'll ring around.'

I put my shoes down, took off my uniform and allowed myself to fall back onto my bed. The pain in my stomach was stronger than I wanted to admit to. Somehow, the bottle of salts had ended up on my bed. I reached out for it, and then wiped the dust off the glass with a tissue. My mother's voice came back to me, '*If* you want to ...' she had said. I checked my watch, and then I googled Harriet's old market stalls.

They still existed, and now they were a bed and breakfast too.

17

Beyond the city, the roads seemed to lengthen and widen. The kilometres clocked up, and so did the time, and then before I knew it, the highway opened into that part of my history where the trees were as tall as the sky. The radio station went from chitchat and a light playlist to scratchy white noise, and when it finally slipped out of range, it put me in mind of that first time my father and I had travelled back from the hospital alone. We had sat in similar white noise for kilometres before either one of us thought to turn the radio off. As an adult, that same sound assaulted my ears so much that it brought home just how numb we must have all once been. I turned the radio off and opened my window. Rushing wind filled my silence. Trees passed. I hit a hundred and ten, maybe a hundred and fifteen on the speedometer.

And then there I was, in amongst the streets I used to know. I was driving and not stopping, looking out of my window as if my window were a picture frame or a television screen. The streets were as vast as they ever were, and for a small moment, I had a sense of something lost. I remembered my long Christmas without Emma. I remembered the trampoline, the cigarettes and my yearning to find in Harriet something of the mother I already missed. Beyond Christmas, I remembered the regular turn of Friday nights, how I used to walk past Harriet's house, watching through lit windows and open doors as she and Samuel prepared for their suddenly popular market stalls. I could still picture it—Harriet wrapping hand-kilned plates and vases in delicate ribbon while Samuel packed boxes in the corner of the carport and filled trestle-tables to the brim with scented soaps, salts, artworks and other 'For Sale' things.

Weekend after weekend they opened that carport to the world. People walked in and then back out carrying clay trinkets or seedlings potted in paper. On Saturdays and Sundays, I wandered the garden and garage as if I too were the child of any tourist now drawn to our town. I played on the grass and dangled from the smooth branches of a fig tree. I touched paintings while Harriet and Samuel mingled with a constantly shifting crowd.

It was a bright morning when Harriet finally found me in amongst her stalls. She said, 'Grace, how are you all? How's your sister?' Then, when I couldn't get my words out, she asked, 'Would you like to work the counter today?'

From then on, I manned her register as best I could. People came to the table. I took their purchases and their notes. I rang the till and scooped out fistfuls of five and ten and twenty cent pieces taking extra care to place the change gently into the palms of my customers' hands. It was nice, this incidental touching of people's skin.

That was how it was: the boxes in the corner, the tables inside the carport, the people coming and leaving, the sound of coins at the checkout. Then, in the evenings, after the markets closed and after she paid me my wages for the day, Harriet and I sat on her front step and mapped out the sky. Sometimes she made herself a cup of tea, and me a warm Milo, every freckle of malt-powder dissolved without me having to ask. Other times, she gave me soup. It was tasty, this soup, different to my mother's avgolemono—thicker and chunkier—yet still as comforting. I remembered always sipping small and satisfying spoonfuls.

Now, as I drove past Harriet and Samuel's old place, I could see that baby olive trees had since grown into sturdy groves and that grapevines and passionfruit vines now grew along all the boundaries. Out the front, the garden was woollier and more coastal than I remembered, filled with soft pale shrubs instead of Harriet's roses. Painted signs advertised plums and apricots, crafts, a bed and breakfast and the art market, which still operated on the weekends just as it did when I was small. It was early, half an hour or so before the till would start ringing. The stalls were not yet fully set up, but there were a few people working. A woman placed crafts on a trestle table. A gardener drove through with tools and plants in the back of a trailer. Someone arranged a painting onto a display easel.

While I waited, I drove to other parts of town. Neighbours were still acres from one another. Homes were still set a lot further from the road than I had since become accustomed to. It surprised me how much space Emma and I had once occupied, and as I drove along all those familiar streets, I thought how contained William had seemed, kicking his ball across the suburban roads. Here whole ovals made up front gardens. A boy like William could have torpedoed the footy as hard as he liked and still not have passed centre square.

Along my street, those front gardens occurred amongst pockets of bushland that were dense and centuries old. The trees looked bigger than I had left them, their trunks looked stronger, and although the dieback disease that had once blackened and charred the occasional tree was now more prominent and widespread than when I was growing up, the shade was still deeper, greener and lovelier than I ever remembered.

My old house had a shine it didn't have before. Gone were the splintered panels and the rusty sheets on the roof. Gone was the concrete driveway with the dark oil stains. Old bronze-coloured flyscreens and sliding doors had been ripped out and replaced. Windows I used to look out of had since been reset against varnished timber frames. Wrapped all the way around the front of the house was a veranda, and on this veranda were pot plants, hanging baskets and a lounge styled with the kinds of blankets and plump pillows that came straight out of a decorating magazine. A glass of water sat idle on the ground. A book turned pages in the breeze. Would things have been different if this was the house we lived in? Surely here my father would not have cracked his fist through bedroom doors, other doors would not have slammed at ten past one in the morning, and I would not have woken to the sound of tyres screeching down the road. The people who lived in my home now—they were not farmers or construction workers. They were a relaxing family, an at-ease, on-holiday family. It was all I could do not to knock on their door and say, 'I'm home. I'm here. Do you recognise me?' I had to push myself to keep driving.

At the lake, not too far down the road, I finally found the courage to step out of the car. I stood on the wooden jetty and stared out across the thrombolites in the same way people on tour buses stare out at amazing things. It was chilly and sunny and cold all at once, and then, of course, because this was Harriet's place and Samuel's too, and because the strangest and most beautiful things always seemed to happen when the three of us came here, a leaf picked up in the breeze and curled through the air in that haphazard way, and then the trees rustled, and I noticed, on the one hand, all the planting that had been done since the fuss with Emma and me, and on the other, how low the water levels had become. Even so, misty threads of oxygen still bubbled up just like they did when I was small. The lake was golden, but the threads beneath the surface were as blue as the morning Samuel first pointed them out to me.

There were no cars, no voices, no electrical motors belonging to air conditioners and other such things, and in the absence of overlaying noise, the only thing that remained was the sound beneath the sound. They weren't just birds chirping, for example, but rather splendid blue fairy-wrens. Random rustling was not random at all, but a bobtail rushing through the scrubs. There was a sharpness to the air, a clarity that was missing in the city. Now and then, I heard a kangaroo, another bird in the bushes, and the sound of water running. If I stood still, I could hear the hum of insects. It made me restless, even here where I thought I would come for rest.

I played with loose debris that had blown onto the jetty. I picked up a couple of tiny stones that maybe a child had left behind, and then I let them slip back out of my fingers again. My skin grew salty. If it hadn't been for Harriet and Samuel back then, I don't know what would have become of me. Harriet was a little bit of this water and a bit of the banks. She was part of the trees and part of the sky. More than my mother, more than anyone, Harriet was the one I sought whenever I wanted someone to speak to. She was always there when I needed her. At a time when life made it hard to know what love and family was meant to be, Harriet made sure that I was okay. For all that had made me lonely, for the simultaneous emptiness and crowdedness of my own house, for every school friend I missed during the holidays, for the parties I stopped being invited to, for all that and more, for my fears too, what I remembered most was the way Harriet flicked the switch on her kettle, as though tea or milk in one of her scalloped cups was all it took to make everything alright.

HARRIET

18

One thing we always tell parents at the hospital is this: make sure the sibling at home has support—an aunty-type will do, a grandparent, a trusted neighbour, someone who can simply step in and care and comfort while the swirls of time begin to occupy the world you once knew. That's what Harriet was to me. That's what I always knew she would be. The more I worked at her market stalls, the more the trust I had imagined manifested into something real. I knew Harriet and Mum chatted to one another over the phone, and that Mum increased her reach to me through the care she asked Harriet to give. I knew too, that Dad didn't mind Harriet after all—other than the 'hippy, greeny things' she did. It made him proud, he said, to see me work. It was good, he added, so long as when the summer finished, I refocused my mind back to school.

That summer, Harriet became my centre. My routines shifted and settled. I worked at her stall. I counted customers' change. She stirred the dots out of my Milo and made me soup. Harriet was everything that my father, without my mother, was not. She was neat for his dirt, organised for his chaos, calm for his temper, considered, careful, the kind of woman who dusted the grooves in her front door and kept fresh flowers in crystal vases. She was eloquent while dad was colloquial. She had a city voice in our county town, but nonetheless it was a knowing voice, one that could somehow locate my mother and sister in the wards and rooms of the hospital.

At Harriet and Samuel's, nothing was out of place. It was easy to feel a sense of order. Light and breeze always seemed to stream through open windows, and what I noticed most was the absence of things. There were no kayaks on the living room floor, no dusty pamphlets or newspapers on the kitchen bench and no dishes in the sink. Equally, though, there were no family portraits, no snapshots held in silver frames, no albums lying around. Instead of family, Harriet and Samuel displayed art. On a shelf where typical photos would normally take pride of place, there was a clay sculpture of a book wrapped in a padlocked chain. Above the mantel hung a painting of an elderly man, seated with his business shirt half tucked-in, half ruffled and his head mostly outside of the shot. On another wall, in quite a different style, there was a hanging quilt, hand-stitched, six squares across, seven down, and full of different patterns and textures—the first a burgundy silk and the last crocheted from white wool.

I said, 'I like your quilt,' and 'I like your painting,' and Harriet told me that she had made both, that her quilting was like a diary she carried around. She said this square of fabric was her ballgown from when she was in high school, and that one was the t-shirt she wore on the day she first moved out of home. Here was her first-ever nurse's uniform, her wedding veil, a sarong from India, a handkerchief embroidered with orange thread that she purchased in Corfu, a collection of her long-ago-husband's ties, a baby's blanket for the baby she didn't get to have, and then one for the baby that this same husband—a man named Bertrand—fathered much later.

I said, 'What do you mean?'

She replied, 'The whole point is to thread a story. Each square is a paragraph. Each stitch joins one part of the narrative to another, but the narrative doesn't disappear once the pages turn.' She said that she never read her history in the same way people read books, that she couldn't order from one page to another. That it made more sense to lay everything bare and all at once.

'How old were you when you moved out of home?' I wanted to know. And 'What were your parents like?' And 'Who was it in your family that my mother said was Greek?'

Then, because I was thirteen, and the sparks of romance were only just beginning to hold my interest, I also asked, 'Did they like the boy who took you to the ball?'

Harriet said she was seventeen, that the boy was nice, and that her parents were as approving and disapproving as parents can be. He was the kind of boy your tooth ached for, like having a crush or being in love, but in the end, nothing ever came of it. Really, it was just an innocent little thing.

I touched the sarong, and then also the handkerchief. I said, 'My mum has a saying about toothaches and love,' and Harriet looked at me and told me that her own mother was English-born but that her heritage was very mixed. Somewhere along the line she had Romani blood, Turkish blood, and one much-loved Greek grandfather, who migrated in the end not from my mother's Aegean, but from the Ionian Sea. Being Romani and Turkish and Greek though, was not something Harriet's parents often talked about—at least not back then—and so sometimes it happened that she said a phrase that someone else recalled from their own upbringing, or a superstition matched, or a dish was familiar, but there was no record, nothing to say that yes this was where it all came from. Absorbed: that was the word she used. One culture absorbed another. Even the name on her birth certificate—the 'Arete' which nodded towards her grandfather's 'Ari'—no longer matched the Harriet she learned to go by. It was better, everyone thought, even as they all migrated once more from Britain to Australia, just to blend in. Harriet touched the fabrics I had touched—the sarong and the handkerchief— and then she told me that these fabrics, they were not heirlooms nor links to her heritage in the same way other immigrants displayed cross-stitched tokens of their past, but rather touristy gifts, purchased on the only holiday she ever had.

'Can you imagine?' she asked, 'knowing so little, you learn your ancestry in gift shops and tours?'

I shook my head, because my mum still had her mother's blankets and rugs safe in that large wooden chest, still spent winters practising the tapestry crafts of her village, still took me to church and still peppered her sentences with mixtures and translations of words. But I also nodded, because something of my mother's history was already slipping from my grasp.

We got along, Harriet and me. She taught me to draw. She gave me envelopes and letter paper and encouraged me to write to my sister.

She liked storytelling, and so did I. She liked painting, sewing and craft. Her artworks, she said—her own and the ones she purchased—were collections of personal histories. They were cracks in the footpath, metaphoric scars on skin and lives etched on people's faces. They were reminders of what once existed. At Harriet and Samuel's, I was always kept busy, always distracted, always prompted into finding something to make sense of the time that passed between now and whenever it was that Emma and Mum would finally come home.

Harriet's place soon melded almost into an extension of my own, and for a little while at least, life seemed to settle in the same way as sand settles both before and after a storm. But then, just as everything seemed to be good and routine once more, an empty syringe appeared on the hard metal of Harriet's kitchen sink. A measuring cup came, a glucose monitor, and a small sharps bin, which Harriet and Samuel kept angled 'just so' between the breadbasket and the block of knives in order to keep the hazard symbol out of sight. Harriet began sorting pills into little date bubbles. She cleaned cupboards and made sandwiches and sorted pills as though all these chores were one and the same.

In an old outdoor laundry that had also been fitted with kitchen items, she tied herbs into bundles and hung them upside down from the rafters, or else she leavened bread and deep-fried tiny balls of dough that she later drizzled with honey and cinnamon. I ate these balls by the plateful. The dough reminded me of my mother's *loukoumádes*, and when I said so, Harriet explained that actually she had found the recipe in a magazine, that her own mother had never cooked like that, but that perhaps—she hoped—someone else in her family once did. In this same kitchen, Harriet collected jars of lake water, which she lined along the windowsill and evaporated into pretty salt crystals. She made soaps and flower-scented oils. She brewed dried herbs and old beef bones into pungent, unappealing broths. The broths were for Samuel, but the donuts were for me.

For his part, Samuel was so much slower and more pensive than when I first met him. He repeated things, forgot things. He slept for hours at a time and yet found himself breathless, puffed and tired. Sometimes I thought of the way he and Harriet used to be when Emma and I visited the lake, how lovely Harriet was, how she chased after us with our left-behind shoes, and how easily she befriended my mother. I thought also of their conversation, and the way my mother had said—honestly and vulnerably—just days before everything changed, 'What is it that you two have? What made you last the distance?'

Harriet had raised a melancholy smile. 'I've had my fair share,' she replied. It hadn't seemed important back then, but in her home where I had since spent most of my days, it bore a significance that I wanted to understand.

Whenever I was with Harriet and Samuel, time seemed at once to gallop and stand still. If Harriet wasn't cooking, she was painting. If she wasn't painting, she was gardening. If she wasn't gardening, she was preparing for her market stall. It was part of her, this stall, but it was also somehow a part of all of us. It maintained us. Harriet bundled soaps into groups of three and tied them together with string. She planted baby olive trees into pots out the back. Samuel moved from the laundry to the carport, and as he fashioned the soap bundles into attractive shop-displays, he talked about oil that would come in five or fifteen years. I found myself helping out too, but instead of elongating time, like Samuel did, I tried to shorten it. Every day I crossed a calendar square off the back of my homework diary. I painted, because painting gave me a visible difference between beginning and end. I sent Emma letters and drew comic strips for her and then, while I waited for the colouring she would send in return, I sat by Harriet's tiny olive trees and willed the branches and roots grow. There, in amongst those plants, I found a spider I liked to watch. Sometimes I poked it gently with a fallen leaf or a broken flower stem. It interested me, the way it would scurry away. It interested me also when I found it curled inward. It didn't move at all, but rather it remained closed, its legs hunched, head over abdomen, its time complete.

'I know my heart,' Samuel told Harriet on the day I found a wad of torn and unsigned consent forms in the compost bin. 'I know my heart,' he repeated, and it stuck with me, what a strange thing this was to say.

'What I want,' he insisted with a frankness that seemed quite out of sync with the way I thought their affection for one another worked, 'is to accept death in a quiet and dignified way.'

Harriet whispered words that were too low for me to hear.

'I can't live like that,' Samuel explained, 'I can't,' and when Harriet didn't reply, he pulled her into his arms and hugged her for a very long time. He said, 'I am not unhappy. I am not.'

I watched a different spider from a distance. It crept to a shadowy corner. I crept too, closer to Samuel, and closer to a conversation belonging only to the adults. What I understood was that Samuel needed treatment of some kind or another, but unlike Emma, who had no choice, he was refusing everything medicine could do for him. There Harriet was, a former nurse, well-versed in scalpels and syringes, and there he stood, obstinate, the love of her life, rejecting everything she once took for granted.

Samuel's kidneys, they were failing. Without a transplant, he would need dialysis for the rest of his life. Without dialysis, he had days or weeks or months left. It would be rapid when it came—a bedridden fade into toxicity—but it would also be kind. That was what Harriet told Samuel when she finally gave up trying to convince him otherwise. It would be without those bright lights, without his body accessed and cut and ripped, and without those cold white rooms.

I dropped something when I heard this: a notebook, a pencil, a twig, I can't remember. I was in the garden, and Harriet was on her patio chair. I dropped something, and she looked at me. 'I'm sorry,' she quickly said, and when I didn't reply, she added, 'It's not the same. Your sister. She's better off for those cold rooms. I promise you, it's not the same.'

But to me, it *was* the same. Love was responsibility. It was my mother bathing us, making dinner and listening to our stories. It was the way Harriet looked at Samuel, the way she yelled at him to put the ice-cream back and take the yoghurt instead. Love was the green of Harriet's garden, the mornings she spent watering. It was my mother rushing Emma to hospital. It was the feel of Emma's port beneath her ribcage and her mouth puffed and stretched with the dry retch that came from her nausea. It was the basin chockfull with horrible yellow acid. Love was my mother wearing gloves and drawing water into a pill-loaded syringe. Love was Emma, this little thing with a visibly racing pulse and the kind of tears that came not from crying, nor from the experiences that had once affected me when I was her age, but from the violence that had burst within her. And then of course, it was me, waiting, hundreds of kilometres away. It was all these things because love was what we did to draw together once more. Love was caring; that's what I had concluded.

And then, just like that, Samuel scrambled this up. He was no longer simply the man who held his love's hand. He wasn't going to be jabbed with needles and catheters. He didn't need to live like that.

Harriet stood up. She sprinkled little balls of fertiliser onto her olive plants. She grabbed the hose, pulled it taut, and began to spray each tree as though spraying trees was the only thing keeping her calm. She looked tense. The hose looked tense. Everything about her was slightly on edge. The soil inside the pots grew black and spongy. The excess water streamed down and out onto the grass. I thought of Emma's forehead, the way we used to pull her fringe out of her eyes. Love was her losing that fringe and gaining instead multiple scars on the base of her spine.

'*Emma* lives like that!!' I shouted. 'She lives like that because *she* loves *us*.' That's what love was to me. There was no other choice, no other way to express such a thing. Mum and I clung, and Emma gave *us* hope. We fought, and we made her fight. And yet, there he was, Samuel, loving Harriet but asking her to let him go.

19

As summer ended, the edges of the lake grew scratchy and bony once more, the thrombolites became whiter and more exposed, and the birds began to sing with the coming rain. Yoghurt, Samuel joked, was no compromise for ice-cream. Multiple check-ins on a dialysis machine was not how he envisioned his old age. Two minutes of the breeze on his face far outweighed a year or more of what medicine could buy. And so, after a while, a steady acceptance settled down on us all. Samuel began to look a little uncomfortable, his feet swelled and his hours no longer split neatly into day and night, but rather cycled in irregular waves. He dozed and woke, dozed and woke, yet at the same time, he still got up in the mornings, he still ate breakfast, and he still grabbed his binoculars and the small tape player with which he'd once recorded chirping sounds. The only difference now, was that he chose to leave his camera at home.

At the lake, Samuel wedged his tape player between the branches of a tree. He pressed play and sat back. 'Look!' he implored as everything filled with the wildlife that answered his birdcall. 'Arete, look! Grace, come see!' He touched the leaves on the trees. He took his shoes off and felt the wood on the jetty. He breathed as if he was breathing the whole lake in.

Harriet did not say much. What was there to say? Instead she sketched as she often did. Or else she brought a square or two of fabric along, a fine needle and a thread, and while Samuel watched the birds flutter across the water, she neatly stitched those squares one onto the next. The fabric came from old clothes, tablecloths and pillowcases. It alternated—something from Samuel, something from her—and it occurred to me that Harriet was journaling a whole new story in the form of a quilt again.

On one of those days, Samuel told me that the thrombolites were oxygen and that they pointed to the place life came from and also to the place it went. We were lucky, he added, lucky to live where we lived and breathe what we breathed. 'Can you feel that?' he asked, sweeping his hands across the sky and all the waters. 'Can you, Grace?' He took another deep breath in. I did too. The air was as icy as Emma's room at the hospital when we first arrived but fresh and clean and without any discernible scent. I breathed as deeply as Samuel did. 'Can you feel it?' he repeated. 'Look below the surface. Can you see those tiny strings of oxygen rising?'

'No,' I said.

'Look harder,' he replied, 'Deeper into the water.'

For the first time, I saw that blue strings of oxygen really did rise to the surface. There was a clear bubbling.

Samuel took another gulp of that crystal air. Harriet put her patchwork aside. She grabbed a small glass jar out of her handbag, laid herself flat on the jetty and reached down to the surface of the lake where she skimmed that jar like a boat amongst those ripples and filled it full of water.

Those last days of summer, we spent almost every day on that jetty. We watched those birds, and we breathed that oxygen as though it simultaneously gave us time and occupied time. Harriet sat right by Samuel's side, stitching yet another square onto her new quilt and collecting her lake-water.

Then autumn's sun-moths started to hatch again. They fluttered like ripped paper cast against the sky. They were brief, and they were colourful. Samuel barely took his eyes off them. The lake deepened, the dew came, the grass turned green and the mushrooms bloomed.

On the first of April, Harriet burned a solitary white candle on the windowsill above her kitchen sink, but when I asked her why she did this, she remained quiet, keeping, at least for the time, her story to herself. Palm Sunday passed without my mother and without Emma, and therefore it also passed without the crosses in my mother's vases, without the boiling dye smell and without the smoky promise of church candles and takeaway boxes.

Samuel weakened, and then weakened some more, and then finally, surprisingly, he said he would give peritoneal dialysis a go.

The roads to the city that day were heavy with the smell of prescribed burns and rain.

Over the next few days, while Samuel and Harriet attended their own myriad of appointments, I sat on Emma's hospital bed and helped her make Easter hats out of cardboard vomit bowls. We painted those hats and glued them full of pompoms, flowers and ribbons. Then, while fluorescent liquid scored through Emma's veins, a consultant came to say that there was good news. As we sprinkled glitter over the top of wet glue, he reminded me of the blood test I took the last time I came and told us both we were as close a tissue match as siblings could possibly be. I was Emma's safety net, her cushion if ever she were to fall. If Emma ever needed it, I had the exact bone marrow that could save her life. My mother wept when she heard this, the IV robot beeped, a nurse came, and Emma cried, 'My throat is yucky!' right before she regurgitated the sticky saliva she no longer properly made.

While all this went on, I counted thirty steps from Emma's room to the kitchen where the kettle was, ten spare mugs in the cupboard next to the fridge, and four people praying in a corner. I saw David, the boy in the bathrobe, all over again. He was making hot chocolates for his family. They were all there—his mum, dad and even his little brother—waiting and chatting as though they were in their own home and not in a hospital. Then the little brother said something, and the whole family grew louder and more boisterous. 'Snake! Snake!' David teased, slithering his hand through the air, and while the parents both laughed, the brother sulked in that half-joking, half-annoyed way.

This was the first time I really paid any attention to the brother at all. He held the remote control in one hand. He sat on the floor next to the coffee table, and while he waited for his hot chocolate, he switched through the same three television channels as obsessively as I counted the minutes required to make my mother a cup of tea. In the same way as he found comfort in the disjointed drone and colour of a constantly changing screen, I counted twelve teaspoons in the drawer, two burning splashes across my fingers and sixteen rooms on the ward.

My mother smiled when I handed her the tea. She sat on the edge of Emma's bed, and as she sipped slowly with an open leaflet of something or another laid out in front of her, Emma and I played and sang nursery rhymes. Emma had seven colouring books and four tubes of plastic animals. There were two Barbie dolls, three small packets of Lego and twenty-nine pages to her protocol.

Inside that protocol, I found five phases to her treatment. Almost three were crossed off in that same way as I had crossed squares off my homework calendar. Between this hospital trip and the end of the next phase, there would be thirty-nine more needles, three trips to theatre, fifty-eight tablets and eight different chemotherapies, but then, in little over seventy-two days, Emma would finally come home. That's what it said: phase five was a you-are-free-to-go stage.

'Mum,' I said, 'does this mean Emma will be finished soon?'

Mum looked over the top of her tea towards the protocol page I was referring to and shook her head. She said treatment would continue for a few more years. She said that in the last phase, a phase called 'Maintenance', Emma would still need hospital, though not as often as before. And then she said, 'But, yes, we *will* be coming home.'

There was one cat quilt on Emma's bed, and two waffle-weave blankets. Emma draped a blanket over her head and created a trail that reached the floor.

'Ooh,' the nurse said as she walked in with a plastic tray full of night medicines. 'What a pretty bride you are.'

'I'm not a bride,' Emma said, twirling that blanket into a long woolly ponytail. 'I'm Rapunzel.'

That evening, after my mother went to have a shower, Emma fell asleep curled against me, that same Rapunzel hair stretching from the tip of her head all the way down to the foot of the bed. She was so bony and light; there was hardly anything left of her. I lay still for a long time, not daring to move. I could hear my mother's slippers shuffling back through the hallway and towards the room. I could hear chatting too: David's mother and mine, both freshly showered, holding toiletries and talking about bone marrow matches and non-matches in the same way other people talked about television shows and Tupperware. Emma snored lightly and huskily. Her mouth was slightly ajar. Her milk teeth, even in the dark, were splashed and spotted with the sepia-coloured stains that came from the mouthwash she had been prescribed, but her breath was as clean and as minty as toothpaste. I turned to the window and to the shapes and lights which moved whenever something large like a bus or a truck went by on the street one level above our basement ward. From what I could hear and understand, David had relapsed, but his brother—Nate—was not his match. 'If Nate were allowed,' David's mother said, 'he would transplant his every cell into David himself, but he and David … the thing is … he and David … everyone knows … they are chalk and cheese, and night and day.'

My mother said, 'What happens now?'

'We wait and hope.'

Emma's IV robot beeped. The lights, though dimmed, had a green and yellow tinge. The conversation shifted to the advice that other people pushed upon both my mother and David's mother. Their voices rose and fell over past life karmas, sugar-free diets and the power of positive thinking. Then Mum shuffled into our room and placed her toiletries back into her overnight bag. She slept on a series of three chairs, which she fashioned into the kind of bed travellers make in snowed-in airports. Although I wasn't technically supposed to stay, I stretched out next to Emma, cuddling her in the best way I knew how.

In the morning, the fairy garden just outside the ward came alive with hidden Easter eggs, hot cross buns and men dressed in life-sized rabbit suits. The children paraded their handmade Easter hats. One after the other, they walked in a line, all of them attached to their IV robots, some wobbling and others limping. We walked too—the siblings and the parents—and no one spoke of medicines or tumours or the sterile rooms on the other side of those heavy doors. Instead we fawned over our hats and costumes. Then somebody said something or another, and Emma giggled the kind of giggle that was both genuine and part of the script she had learned. The adults made silly jokes and the children giggled. They shrugged their little shoulders up and hid their laughs behind the palms of their hands.

Emma did not want to parade her hat. She had painted it pink and decorated it with ribbon and tissue cut into a paper chain of dancing ballerinas. It was pretty, and I was proud of her, but she stood there, quietly shaking her head. The play-lady said in a soft sing-song voice, 'Come Emma. It's your turn,' but Emma simply pursed her lips and handed me the hat. I crouched and let her dress me up. He fingers felt little and light against my forehead, but she was warm with her touch. She took her time, tilting the ballerina hat from here to there until finally she had it just right.

'Will you come with me?' I asked, reaching for her hand, but she remained stiff with her arms by her sides and her head bowed into an unlockable private space. In the end, I took the walk alone. I went from one end of the garden to the other. I played my part. I knew my script too. The play-ladies, the bunnies, the nurses with their baskets of never-ending eggs, were all there to shine a smile on our faces, and we shone a smile right back.

The winning hat belonged to David. He had made a rocket ship out of a urinal tube. It was metallic and silver and black. Spent toilet rolls functioned as turbo jets. Toilet paper, painted orange and red, burst like fire out of the ends.

Back home, Harriet caressed the inside of Samuel's arm and ran her fingertips alongside a new, medically created fistula. It seemed so abject, this bump—as unnatural as my sister's port. Between this and the catheter that was attached to his abdomen, Samuel was suddenly unfamiliar to me. The medicines bloated him, his lymph nodes grew fat and visible, and his face and gut looked as swollen and as slippery as water balloons. 'Will you?' he said to Harriet, nodding towards a bag filled with clear liquid. As Harriet grabbed the bag and attached it to Samuel's catheter, I saw an acquiescence in him I hadn't seen before. Clean liquid went into his abdomen via the catheter, and then later, waste flushed out in much the same way. It was very mechanical, exactly what he had hoped not to have.

Samuel complained that the fluid was cold. He wanted to know why it couldn't be warmer? And what would happen if he zapped it in the microwave for a bit? Same-same—that was what he wanted—a match for his body temperature, and no more sensation.

'Same,' I told him, 'that's what I am to my sister. A perfect match.'

'She's lucky to have you,' he said as he infused the fluid he needed through his catheter. For forty-five minutes I sat near him as he waited his dialysis out nearby. He did not speak. There was a rash on his face—sunburn because despite what the doctors said about his photosensitivity, he was determined to be in the sun, to feel it, to live just a finger of life fuller if it could not be longer.

It didn't occur to me to leave him be or go home. By that stage, I was as much a part of his and Harriet's house as I was my own. I was comfortable, and Samuel didn't seem to mind, so I sat, just as I used to sit with Mum and Emma in the winter, but instead of watching my mum with her tapestry, I watched Harriet sew together more squares of fabric for a new wall quilt. She stayed close to Samuel, and she fashioned these squares not into rows and columns as she had done before, but into small groups of two or three. They looked like pieces of a jigsaw, all disjointed like that, and when she set them aside they formed an odd pile. Towards the end of Samuel's infusion time, Harriet prepared for him a footbath. She placed a large tub in the basin of the bathroom sink and poured in water, oils and the salt crystals that she had previously collected from the lake. She paddled her hand in gentle swirls.

'Why do you that?' I asked. 'Why do you use the lake salt?' And then, without waiting for a reply, I said, 'Harriet, do you believe in the things people say?'

She replied, 'What things?'

'Like karma makes illness, and we're only given what we can handle, and oh you're so strong, and all these experiences, they are lessons, and perhaps things are not meant to be.'

'Who has said those things to you?'

'People,' I shrugged.

For a small moment, the only sound between us was the running of the tap. Harriet said, '*People* are insensitive.' Then she said that the painting in the lounge room—the one of the man whose head was not in the shot—that painting was the very first painting she had ever completed for anyone other than herself. Samuel commissioned it. That was how they met, and how they fell in love. He was married. She was separated but, as unhappy as Samuel was at the time, he was fair and square with someone else. *People* said those karma and not-meant-to-be things back then too. 'Forget people,' Harriet maintained even though I wasn't quite sure what she was connecting. 'People are cruel.'

Harriet quietened. She swirled the water in the tub, shook her hands, and absentmindedly rubbed the nails on her left hand with the thumb of her right. Then she looked at me almost in the same way as my mother did on the day she told me to never put myself in a situation where I depended on a man. 'Firstly,' she said, 'There is no such thing as karma. Karma is what people say when they haven't the foggiest idea what to say. And secondly, don't look back.' As she turned the tap off, she added one last piece of advice, 'Always,' she said in direct opposition to my mother's *never*, 'take care of your heart.' This was why she put the lake salt in Samuel's footbath. It wasn't just because it made his muscles feel less sore. It wasn't something mystical or cultural that she was trying to emulate. One day, she promised, she would tell me the whole story, but for now, all I needed to know was that the lake was where she and Samuel learned to hear the beats and rhythms of their hearts.

20

And then what?

Then Samuel died, and everything that had propped me up fell away once more. We wore black and we watched the sadness wash over Harriet's face. I sat at her dining table after all her guests had gone, after days had passed. At the kitchen sink, she squeezed the tea out of yet another one of those instant not-anything brands, and when I said, 'Are you okay?' she turned to me and cried because Samuel would never have drunk anything so bland.

'I'm tired,' she said. 'I'm fed up.'

'You're tired?' I asked.

'Sometimes I wonder when it's going to be my turn.'

'Your turn?'

'It's like that, you know. It's just the next thing.'

I stared at her, and when I didn't respond quickly enough, she added, 'I used to wait for him at the hospital. He'd drive in sometimes, on Fridays usually. I'd wait for him. I'd wait out the front. Seven in the morning, after my shift, and I would wait for him.'

And then she said, 'I probably shouldn't be telling you this.'

'Harriet, do you remember when I was upset about—'

'People,' she interrupted, because she always seemed to know what I was thinking.

'Yes, people,' I said.

'Someone had told you that karma made illness.'

'My mum,' I said, 'someone had told my mum. And you sat with me and told me all about you and Samuel and the painting you made of him. You said he was married. And that people were cruel, and that karma was rubbish ...'

'It is,' Harriet said.

'Harriet ...'

'What are you thinking?' she asked.

I shook my head. Then I said, 'Will you finish the story you promised me?'

Harriet went to the fridge, poured herself a water, poured me one too, boiled the kettle once more and asked if I wanted a hot drink.

'No,' I said, but she heated milk and served up a plate of biscuits nonetheless.

She told me a little that day, and a little the day after. The whole time she spoke, she kept her hands busy. She pinned together the groups of fabric that she had sewed when Samuel was still alive. Then she unpinned them, shifted them around and pinned once more. When she was satisfied with the orientation of the squares, she began to sew them permanently into place. I learned her story over those days, but I also learned a lot more later, and a lot from my mother. Sometimes I wondered if I had since layered my adult story onto Harriet's, but either way, what I carried was this: before Samuel, Harriet was married to a man named Bertrand, who had seemed nice enough at first, but really wasn't. It took Harriet years to accept this, and then another lot of years of facing her loneliness and the damage it had done to her esteem, and it was only later—after she went back to nursing school and after she had worked long enough for the stretchers in the emergency room to have taken their toll—that she met Samuel. She had gone back to study once more, but this time towards an art and textiles course, and he had come along with a friend to her first exhibition, which was a joint event with the other students from her school. She couldn't say why he was there or who he was supporting, but in amongst it all, they got talking, and he asked if she did portraits.

She said, 'I don't know. Not really,' because all she had attempted up until then were still lifes and the odd copy from a photo.

He looked at her and he said, 'It's odd, I know, and I wouldn't normally ...' His face went a little pink.

And so, she said, 'Okay, I'll try.'

They were both living in the city at the time. She used to wait for him after her night shift, and he would drive in, and she would wait, and it wasn't anything at first, just a painting commission. He would sit, and she would do these pencil sketches to get an idea of what she could paint—hundreds of them, each time he came—and when she finished, he would thank her and go to work.

One thing led to the next. It was a cliché, she knew, but there was no better way to describe it. One thing led to the next and to the next, and all along she grew more and more powerless against it. Samuel hadn't wanted his head in the painting, for example, and when she asked why, he argued that he had always followed the expectations of his intellect— he was a husband, a father, a professional, a businessman. His brain made the choices, he had told her. They were good choices, executive and stable. His head was the boardroom, and his heart the worker that followed whatever it was told to do. 'I don't know my heart,' he had said. 'I don't know my heart,' and so, he sat for her, and Harriet began yet another pencil sketch, different to the ones she had made before, and as she drew him, he talked over the dreams he once packed into dark boxes, and the love that had since faded, and the disappointments along the way. His whole life was one 'do the right thing' after another. Really, it was nothing, just an artist and her subject every morning before their days began, but then she said, 'Unbutton your shirt a bit. Loosen it for me.'

And he said, 'Why?'

'All your life,' she replied, 'the right thing, packed into boxes, like your heart packed into your suit.'

He unbuttoned, loosened, relaxed. More of nothing happened; she painted him, and off he went to work.

Then one rainy morning, when she finally washed a thin layer of paint onto her canvas, he turned to her, and he said, 'Reti, you make me feel so alive.'

No one had called her Reti before, but Reti was closer to her real name than the name she actually went by. On her birth certificate, the letters were not H and A and R and so on, but rather 'Arete', which had always brought to her mind heroic queens and chariots instead of Harriets, and in that moment, she questioned whether the 'e' at the end of her legal name was really as she had always supposed, a lengthening sound, or if in fact it worked in much the same way as Samuel had pronounced it, as an 'i' or a 'y' to sweeten and shorten the vowel. She wondered who it was in her family that had given her such a name and had promptly taken it away, and why the discrepancy, why the plainer, less interesting Harriet over the name she ought to have gone by. Still, she liked the sound of 'Reti' on Samuel's lips, and she liked also the other thing that he had said, the thing about being 'alive'. She had felt what it was between them too, this underlying brewing, but at the same time, her heart was just as packed away as his was, and her brain also did the talking. 'You're married,' she said.

'I'm not *married*,' he replied, and he emphasised the word 'married' as though the vows he once signed had somewhat disenchanted him. 'The romance has gone. It's spent. My wife and I, we're financial partners.'

He sat for her, and she painted, and then he went to work.

He sat for her, and she painted, and then he did not go to work.

'It's not me you want,' she said. 'It's the boy you used to be.'

'It's you,' he told her. 'Ever since I met you.'

Then one thing really did lead to another. He didn't stop it and neither did she. It was odd after all those years to be with someone new. His hair was so white against her pillow, his snoring loud and alien.

They slept and woke and slept, and then, at one point, while they lazed in and out of the newness and confusion of 'was this love?', Harriet reached for Samuel's hand. As she lingered over the bracelet of lines that seemed to join his palm to his forearm, it struck her how honest the inner side of his wrist was, how easily he gave it to her and how vulnerable he seemed to be. She never had that vulnerability before—at work, yes, a vein here to be needled, a space there to draw blood—but in love, no-one had ever given her so much. It was fragile. Love was fragile. Yet there he was, Samuel, allowing her to trace the path of his veins, exposing his wrist to the possibility of loss, relinquishing himself. It wasn't a direct line to the heart for nothing.

He asked, 'What are you thinking?'

She said, 'I know what to do about that painting of yours,' and she sat him down once more, but this time, she asked him to lean forward and a bit to the side, and she had him rest his left arm down near his knee and use his right like a prop between his leg and his jaw. Then she positioned his thumb, index and middle fingers in an L-shape from his jaw-joint to his temple. Effortlessly, as the rest of his fingers fell into curls, his wrist turned towards her. This was what she wanted: he was pensive and thoughtful, preoccupied with what was on his mind, but also open enough so she could see the translucence of those anterior veins.

Oil was her medium. It was soft, forgiving and malleable. When she painted, she always started with a thin wash of an idea, a base which was tonal and shadowy, and which lightened and took shape as she layered one colour on top of another. Samuel's portrait had been a sketchy, diluted underpainting for a lot longer than she expected it to be. He had sat, and she had painted him as he wanted—head outside of the shot, buttons undone and pants all bunched up—and really, there was never anything wrong with the composition, never any reason for Harriet not to progress to the thicker more detailed layers, but at the same time, there was also something never quite right.

All this changed once she modelled him with his wrist exposed.

They did not talk. Harriet wrapped a rag around her finger, dipped it in turpentine and as she wiped away what was uncomfortable and closed and added what had been missing all along, she looked at her own hands by comparison. Her fingers were long and spidery, her palms had interesting fortune lines, her nails were that enviable tapered shape, but her skin was not as soft as Samuel's, and her wrists were not honest. She had spent a lifetime hiding them, moisturising them, cloaking them in gloves, splashing them with paint, trying fruitlessly to bury the visibility of what they showed. There were scars—a knife mark, a hot-oil mark, even a cigarette butt. They looked like chasms, all of them, emptied of wrinkles and colour, and yet not empty at all. Every single one reminded her of what she experienced before Samuel.

Samuel had met her at the hospital on what Harriet later supposed was their first date. She wore a pair of jeans, a plain black top and a set of bangles that she once purchased from a market stall similar to the one she eventually ran herself. It was a Saturday this time, and he drove her all the way to Fremantle port, and a little bit around, just to show her where he was from—not where he lived, but where he grew up.

It was nice, watching the scenery from a moving window: the Federation brick of the buildings; the traffic bridges; the boats—all sorts—everything from container ships to little dinghies; the thick sheep smell; the wool-scouring yard across the northern side of the water; car sales; antique furniture shops.

He wore slacks and a polo shirt, all neatly pressed and tucked in. She teased him about dressing like an accountant even on the weekend, and he reached over to her side of the car and play-pushed her thigh. It was light-hearted and mischievous, just this little 'haha-don't' kind of knock, but it threw her off guard in a way she didn't quite expect. Instinctively, she pressed her hand on that leg. She looked at him, and he looked back too. He was driving, and looking at her, and looking at the road ahead, and also at her leg, and then at her. He said, 'I'm sorry. I didn't mean to upset you. I was playing. I'm sorry.'

She said, 'I know,' because it *was* play and he clearly didn't mean it, but in a way, it threw her more, this sensitivity, and where it came from, and how suddenly out in the open it was. It was awkward then, both of them stuck for words. She felt herself shrink. Was she less for having had the experiences she had? Was she something to be pitied? What was it that Samuel, a married man, was attracted to? Was she vulnerable? Easy? Weak? Would he turn on her too, the way Bertrand once had, or the way everyone else had when they asked, 'But if so, why didn't you leave?'

Samuel took her to a coffee shop on the esplanade side of South Terrace. He ordered Orange Pekoe, which she had never heard of before, and she drank a milky coffee. He said he had another name too—*Samuele*—which came from an Italian heritage, but which his family changed as soon as they stepped off the boat. There they were, talking histories and cultures and showing each other the real names on their driver's licences. They spoke about their upbringings and the length of time in which it took before they called themselves 'Australian'. But did their legs entwine? Did they brush fingers across the table? Did they lean in for a kiss or intimate whisper? Not once. The risk, Samuel said, was too much.

Something bristled in Harriet then: this hidden thing, this feeling like she was not the sort of woman to be proud of. Still, they went to the markets. They waited in long lines for fresh crepes filled with fruit and maple syrup. They bought homemade sweets, and ham-and-salad sandwiches that were still made, despite the fashion, with thick layers of butter, beetroot and shredded lettuce. They drank in west-end pubs and they wandered down to the coast, not to the Roundhouse or to the Maritime Museum, but to Port Beach, windswept and hidden from view. Finally, they found themselves back at her house. She put the kettle on. She asked, 'Tea or coffee?'

But when he replied, 'What do you have?' she looked in her pantry, at the generic Bushells bags and the instant granules, and she didn't know what to say.

'Actually, whatever you're making will do,' he said as he studied the books on her shelf and the paintings on the wall. He had posed for her many times, had visited before, had slept in her bed, but that particular day, it felt as though he was trying to figure *her* out. He touched her wall-quilt—the first one she had made—one square to the next, and when he reached the final square—a baby's blanket—he said, 'Did you make this?'

She came in from the kitchen, holding the jar of sugar in one hand, and when she realised he was talking about the blanket and not the quilt as a whole, she said, 'No.'

◉ ◉ ◉

There used to be whole nights when Harriet would lie by Bertrand and wonder what life might be like if she married a gentler man. She used to image something more civilised than what she had. She used to lie by him and dream of this kinder soul: the heat of his skin, the charge of his arm next to her arm.

And then, there he was, Samuele.

◉ ◉ ◉

Their next time together—the following Friday—Samuel sat on her couch and said something about her being just as closed as he was.

She said, 'What do you mean?'

He confessed that it was hard getting to know her. 'You don't display any pictures,' he said. 'Nothing really. And when I try to start conversations about you, you shut like a shell.'

'I do not,' she said.

'You do,' he insisted, and he pointed to the hanging quilt on the wall as proof.

So, because she didn't quite know how to start with the stories in her fabric art, she showed him what he expected—a photo album—instead. It was a tatty thing, rectangular and bound in olive vinyl that had peeled at the edges. The cover was imprinted with horses pulling hay-carts, rolling hills and pigs grazing in fenced off paddocks. There was a church steeple in the top left-hand corner. The photos inside were unfocussed and haloed in a fuzzy sepia light. Harriet was young then, more attractive than she had ever considered herself at that time. There were pictures of her pinning tulle in her hair, posing next to a brass bed, standing with her groom outside a dark-bricked church. There was a picnic—a large group of friends sharing sandwiches in a field thick with grass and clover, all of them waving to the camera, hair shiny and gleaming in the sun. There was a birthday party too—balloons, streamers, children with their faces smeared with chocolate cake. And finally, there were school pictures—two skinny dark-haired boys in identical checked shorts and tucked-in shirts, posing on the doorstep of their house.

He asked, 'Are these two yours?'

And she shook her head, 'A neighbour's. But we were close.'

'Oh,' he said.

Harriet took her quilt down from the wall then. She draped it over her legs, and as she ran her fingers along the thread, she told Samuel all the things that were difficult to say, all the things she and Bertrand never spoke about. She told him she did have a baby once—a long time ago—but this baby died before he was born. She was eight months along when she lay in that delivery room, the sound of live infants crying all around her, his birth so silent in comparison, not a whimper, no, 'Congratulations he's a boy.' She said his name was Arty and his birthday—*if* he were able to celebrate one—would've been on April Fools, the cruelty of which was never lost on her. She said people didn't know what to say. She was sure they crossed the street to avoid saying anything at all, and so she imagined them talking instead to one another, gossiping with phrases like 'she lost her baby' and platitudes that included nature's mysterious ways, and it was all she could do not to stand in the middle of Hay Street Mall and shout at the top of her lungs that she had not *lost* him, had not misplaced him, had not laid him down at the shops and forgotten which aisle she had left him in.

People were far more forgiving of Bertrand than they were of her.

Technically, that blanket belonged to another woman, to a *friend* of Bertrand's actually, who went on to have the baby Harriet didn't have: a girl this time, with a far more sensible name—Ruth—who was born not in a hospital but in the company of nuns.

People said things then too. They said, 'Men do misbehave.' And 'You need to look after Bertrand, pay him a bit more attention.' And 'Harriet, you're lucky he stayed.' That blanket, insensitively given to her by a neighbour to pass along, was nothing more than a reminder to never look back.

Samuel held *her* hand then. He turned *her* wrist over and back, studied *her* arm. He pointed to the long vertical scar that marked the inside of her wrist, 'What happened there?'

She stared at the tell-tale skin. She said as succinctly and as honestly as possible, 'A long life with Bertrand.'

Samuel caressed the scar, wrapped her in his arms and held her for a long and quiet time. He wiped the hair from her face, his touch so noticeably soft and gentle that Harriet felt the first slip of what could possibly be love. She could all too easily fall, she thought. She could fall head over heels and tumble into love, which was a problem because a love like this would only unearth all that she had worked so hard to forget. And so, for a little while, she found herself in this dual dance, torn ironically between that heart of hers and the reason that resided inside her head.

Driving, it seemed, was the worst. At home there was intimacy, and at the shops or in the cafés there was distance. In those places, the rules were clear, but in the car, particularly on those longer journeys, there was this strange feeling that made Harriet tense. It was always serious— what they talked about—once they started talking: regret and loneliness and Samuel's wife and Harriet's own marriage with Bertrand. And it wasn't just that. Sometimes it felt as if Samuel was somehow stronger, more successful and worldlier than her. It was awful to say, wasn't it? But this was how it was. He knew about Orange Pekoe, he had earned himself a good lot of money, and he had travelled far more than she could ever imagine. He wasn't afraid to do things. He was calmer, more communicative. He never said, 'You don't listen to me,' like Bertrand used to, but rather, 'I don't feel heard.' There was a difference, to her mind, in these two things, and so sometimes she worried about what she was saying, and if her words were up to scratch, or if they sounded educated enough, or whether she was just revealing her own weaknesses. She didn't always want to have a serious conversation. Sometimes it settled her more just to be chit-chatting and carrying on, and so she talked about the spots on the cows in the paddock up ahead or the road markings or what a patient at the hospital said. But then one day, Samuel had tried to say something important—*I left my wife*—and he jumped in midway through her sentence and interrupted her train of thought. Harriet had become so flustered that she continued louder and with more urgency about those cow spots.

'I left my wife,' he said again. 'I asked for a divorce.'

Harriet froze. She wasn't sure what to say. She thought, 'I'm sorry to hear this,' might be appropriate. Or maybe a simpler, 'Oh.' But none of those words truly reflected what it was that burned within her. What did he expect now? Would he push her too far too soon? Did she choose him only because he was unavailable?

'What does this mean?' she asked when she finally spoke again. 'We didn't talk about this. What does this mean?'

Samuel said, 'It's what *I* wanted,' and then when Harriet hesitated to reply, he added, 'I'm not asking for more than what you're willing to give.'

On that same drive, Samuel took Harriet to the lake. She had never seen it before. She hadn't even known it existed. They drove a long way, and when they finally arrived, he took her down to the jetty, and they sat in the silence of those thrombolites for a long time.

'You're like these thrombolites,' he said eventually. 'I appreciate you, hear you, see you. Do you know that? Your quietness is like their quietness. I want to reach in the water and touch you. I want to know what you feel like, and what temperature the water is, and whether you're like coral or like rock. But I know if I reach in, I upset your ecology. And so, I step back and appreciate you from a distance. It is my instinct to get close, but also to stay away.'

That was the kind of love they had. The lake was their place for listening: the two of them and nothing other than a bubbling sound, the slowness of it all, the water lapping.

'You can't touch a thrombolite,' Samuel said. 'You can't walk on it. You can't even get in the water.'

'I know,' Harriet replied, because her instinct was the same. 'I feel it too,' she said. 'But I can't stop the more protective part of me.'

Samuel waited. He waited and waited. He waited for his divorce, he waited for Harriet and he waited until he learned what it was to wait, and then after his marriage was well and truly over, he and Harriet tentatively stepped forward, this time without stepping back.

It was always a little hesitant between them, always like walking on soft, thick grass, but with the memory of a bee sting or a prickle lodged deep in the balls of their feet. They were human too. Samuel was not perfect, and neither was Harriet, and yet slowly but surely, they each relearned their hearts. Harriet didn't have to be a nurse forever, and Samuel didn't need to work in a bank. Samuel was Samuel. He was not Bertrand. People could say whatever they liked. They could call Harriet a homewrecker if they wanted to. They could pretend her child Arty happened for a reason, or wasn't meant to be, or didn't exist in the first place. They could forget he was ever born and turn their faces from her long-ago pain. They could tell her she threw her marriage to the bin, and that she took Samuel's too. They could say whatever they liked. What she knew was this: when she arrived at the lake, when she and Samuel made their sea-change or tree-change or whatever people called it, when they stood on the jetty and looked at those thrombolites and saw them for the ancient egg-like creatures they were, they both understood that there was no reason, no master plan, no anything.

Karma had not caused anyone's sickness: not Arty's, not Samuel's, and for that matter, not Emma's either. There was no karma—not in the way most people understood karma, and certainly not in the checkbox 'you-did-this, now-that-pays' kind of way.

But there was love.

THE ONLY ORDINARY YOU SEE

21

At the jetty, all these years later, something long past seemed to ripple through me in the same way a skimming stone sends waves long after it sinks. It wasn't just Emma and the illness that I could not pin to a timeline. It wasn't Samuel and his breath for this lake or Harriet and her habit of quilting stories into a frame. It wasn't even my mother, gone for what was really just a few short months of my life. It was now also Zoe and work, and the constant feeling that I was sinking through water. It was me and this child that I carried and wanted and also wasn't sure about. A slow-motion watery sound. A rock not only skipping along the surface of a lake, but also hitting the ground and sending sand and sediment upwards in barely perceptible shifts of landscape. What would Harriet do, I wondered. And my mother? And all the other mothers? And Emma? What would Emma say in the late-effect aftermath of the chemical bargains my mother once made on her behalf?

The thrombolites bubbled. Inside my bag, I had the bottle of salts that Harriet had once distilled and given me. It was cold to touch. In a way, its coolness had always reminded me of the coolness of the lake, but I was also now acutely aware that it lacked sound and movement. I stood at the jetty and strained to hear as much of this movement as I could—the bubbling, the leaves of nearby bushes in the breeze, crickets, birds. I wanted to listen just as Samuel and Harriet had taught me to, but instead of the natural world, it was the sound of approaching clip-clopping footsteps and gossipy voices that interrupted and drowned the best of my thoughts.

'Oh, it really is as lovely as you told me it would be,' one woman said.

'But is she okay?' the other asked, referring to a conversation that must have begun some time before.

I turned around a little so as to let the women enter my line of sight. If I had to guess, I would have placed them around my age or younger, but at the same time, they also had this air about them as though their lives were already sorted in a way that somehow eluded me. Both women wore beige, both had their fingernails and toenails painted, and in addition to their tell-tale diamonds on their tell-tale fingers, both were adorned with various chains and gems. They were affluent, the kind of women who spoke with crisp pronunciation and whose conversations involved an endless cycle of pending holidays and household purchases.

The women leaned against the same railings I leaned on and stared out over the lake, but they were chatty and distracted. Each held a glass of white wine, which I presumed they had purchased from the vineyard next door, and although it was still morning, both were flushed in that champagne-breakfast kind of way. One passed her wine to the other while she grabbed a fancy camera out of a satchel. She snapped a shot as if this camera was simply a smartphone or the kind of disposable you purchase in pharmacies or touristy gift stores. Then she promptly put it away and took her wine back.

'Though ...' she continued, elongating the 'though' and pausing as if to enact a break. 'She seems to be coping.'

The first woman shook her head in that what-a-pity kind of way. 'She hardly meets anyone, and then when she does, she picks the worst sorts.'

'It's her own fault. I bought her a gym membership for her birthday. Three months later, she's telling me she hasn't found the time to use it.'

'*I* met Chris at the gym. If she gave it a chance, left the house once a while, she could meet someone like him.'

The women kept talking, this time about their corporate husbands with their corporate jobs and their corporate four-wheel drives they never took off road, and I wondered what Samuel would have said to make them listen to the lake, and then I thought also of Nate and Al-i-son, and whether Alison spoke with the same confident assurance about her own relationship. Half of me wanted to say something, but then the other, more dominant half stayed mute. I walked to the far edge of the jetty, as far from their voices as possible. As I waited for their wine glasses to empty and then for their inevitable retract back to the restaurant, I listened hard for those lake-notes once more.

It was only later, after the women left, and after another walker came— a man this time, out exercising his dog—that I finally heard something closer to what I must have needed all along. He said, 'It's nice, hey,' and straight away, I warmed to that 'hey', and especially to the inflection at the end of his voice.

'Are you from here?' I asked.

He nodded, and then he shook his head. 'Preston Beach.'

In the small talk that came next, I heard other words and phrases I used to know, the kinds of words my dad's friends once drew on. 'Nah, mate,' he said. And, 'Yeah, nah, better down south, hey.' And, 'Have a nice arvo then.' I was only a couple of hours away from the city, but there was a clear distinction between the way the women and this man spoke. Everything about him was different—his syntax, his accent, everything—and it occurred to me that I was nostalgic for words I never thought I would miss.

22

When I was born, I think I fell into my mother's words before I fell into my father's. I knew that *mýti* was nose and *máti* was eye. *Pou eínai to pódi sou?* meant 'where is your foot?' I could count '*éna, dýo, tría*', say the alphabet and sing nursery rhymes, but by kindergarten, just as my English flourished, much of the Greek I had learned fell away. Greek was relegated to a sound I heard only when I was with my mother. It was the language of special occasions, churches and prayers. Greek was the repetition of meaning. It was my name, which my mother said came from the three Graces or the charities, and which I learned was the word *chári* with a 'h' sound or even no consonant sound—Ariti whenever I was in trouble but Hari when Mum was being sweet to me. Greek was learning that I shared this name with Harriet, and that our mothers each changed what we were christened with either phonetically or by definition. It was the language lessons I did at the kitchen table, the scribbles in my early reading books, the translations for 'here is the cat' and 'here is the milk', the copy for copy shifts from Greek letters to English ones and the confusion I always had about where to place the accents on a written word. But Greek was also the inserts that soon began to fill my own sentence structures, *kaliméra* and *kalinihta* instead of good morning and goodnight. Greek was an adjunct that sat so very parallel to the language that came from my dad.

When Mum took Emma to the hospital, she took my at-home words away from me. I used to visit Samuel and Harriet just to imagine something in the region of what my mother might have said. I purposely avoided my father's slang, and so it shocked me now, as I watched the man walk his dog back down along the paths, to feel the same yearning—a yearning I thought was fixed—reorientating itself once more back towards my dad.

I wasn't finished at the lake. Beyond me the lake glimmered in a way that the bottled salts I carried in my handbag didn't. The salts in the lake were fluid, invisible to the eye. The salts, held in glass, were white, rocklike and caked. There was more for me to do, more to put to rest, but also, there was somewhere else I needed to be. I turned around once more, turned my back to the lake and its simultaneous still but swirling energy and began to retrace my steps down along the jetty towards the parklands, the restaurant and then to my car. As much as I had wanted to see the lake once more, I now comfortably drove away from what I had intended, towards something different altogether.

Twenty or so minutes on the road heading south, and I found myself taking the turn towards Nate's old hometown. Preston Beach and Lake Preston were part of the same national park that my town belonged to. Our towns were similar in a way, but also not quite the same. I suppose I could liken them to my mother and Nate's mother and the bond they forged at the hospital, or to Nate and I and the way our paths crisscrossed, but also diverged. The kangaroos here were quite possibly the same as the kangaroos at home, but Nate's lake was always so much more arid than mine. Still, any tourist who would have come for our thrombolites, would have also driven on the bridge that cut over Lake Preston and would have taken a swim in the ocean of Nate's beach. Our towns were part and parcel of the same holiday. Nate's was where the fishermen lived. It was my early playground from a time when my parents were happy. It was short drives, long hours between morning and night, Boxing Days, New Years, picnics, sand in my cheese-and-lettuce sandwiches, the park, grass on my wet legs, driving home, bathers still damp, hair knotty and powdery, eating lollies in the backseat of the car. Preston Beach was the photo of my dad with me. But it was also the years of Christmases after Emma was born, years when we ruptured our routine and instead stayed home. It was where I broke Dad's kayak, and also where Mum, Emma and I often played, without Dad, when

Emma first returned home from hospital. Even so, now as I passed Lake Preston and travelled towards the sea, I felt myself a stranger. The lake was still as salty and dry as I remembered. Deep in the middle there might have been water, but equally that shimmer could have been the reflection of the sun. Here was where Emma, my mother and I came to be tourists ourselves. There was where we swam, played and rested. That was where the caravan park used to be. Now a fancy resort spread across acres of land. I focused on the familiar things: the ongoing smell of something somewhere on a barbecue, or else the galahs and magpies which always seemed to take up so much of the road. A delivery truck pulled out of the resort car park. Kookaburras called from the tips of their branches.

The beach itself was choppy and a little rough, but it was still a pretty beach. I walked along the shore and let the water lap against my toes. A solitary swimmer splashed deeper in the ocean. Up ahead, a fisherman stood with his fishing rod pointed upwards and the line disappearing into the sea. I walked to the tyre groyne and sat in the same spot I sat on the day Dad refused to take the kayaks out. Already the black rubber felt warm to touch and as dusty with sand as it had been that day long ago.

For a little while, as other fishermen cast out or reeled in, I let myself settle into a kind of silence. Beyond me, a family played in the sand. From a distance, they could have easily been a happier version of Mum, Dad, Emma and me. The mother, like my mother, was slim, pretty, olive and dark-haired. The man was fair. The older girl was wiry like I was, and the little one poked her belly out in the same way my sister might have.

One game led to another, and then one more, and then all of a sudden both girls were buried up to their necks. The man shovelled great ridges of sand with those bulldozer hands of his. The woman patted everything lightly. Everyone laughed—they were a laughing family. The children bobbed their heads from side to side in the same way plastic clown-faces move at fairs. Then the eldest wriggled her arms and legs out of the sand. As the girls freed themselves, Dad chased Mum and tapped her at the hip. 'You're it!' he shouted, and she turned around and did the same. She was right in there, energised. The girls ran to the shore and back again. Chase evolved into shell collecting and sandcastle building. The girls pressed shells around a moat. Mum sat with her feet curled beneath her buttocks. She patted the castle down, smoothed the walls. Dad leaned in and pushed sand over the kids.

I took a quick and secret snapshot on my mobile phone. Then I sat back, watched the ocean, watched the fisherman and looked at the photo rather than the actual family in front of me.

The sun grew high in the sky. I sat for some time caught in my own daydreams, but when the shadows shortened completely, I found myself looking at the family again. The adults stood to leave. 'Time to go,' the dad said, but no sooner as his words left his mouth, the youngest girl fled towards the water's edge.

'Two more minutes,' she called, turning back for the slimmest of moments. 'Two more minutes, please.'

In tandem, both adults shook their heads.

I caught snippets of their conversation. 'No ... the answer is no ... it's nearly lunch ... the sun is too high in the sky now ... and anyway soon it'll be time for a nap.'

In a final attempt to have her way, the little one pouted, sat herself on the ground, folded her arms and refused to move.

'The beach is lovely,' Mum consoled, 'but your sister can't stay all day.'

Dad took the girl's hand, and as he gently coaxed her up into his arms, I remembered my own mother's reluctance to let Emma play in the sun. I took a good look at the older girl then. She could have had anything. It could have been other medicines, a fairness to her skin, any sensitivity, dermatitis even, but it didn't matter, because what I heard—*your sister can't stay all day*—took me straight to old conclusions. Was her hair shorter than normal? Did she look familiar? She certainly wasn't a child that I had ever treated on the ward, but I still couldn't shake the desire to know the reasons behind what the mother said.

I stood up at the same time as the family readied to leave, but instead of heading to the carpark like they did, I walked towards the shore. On the way, I collected shells just as the family had earlier. There was nothing particularly special about these shells. They were small and pink and the kind you can find on any Western Australian beach, but at the same time, they were warm from a morning in the sun. I held them for a while, and then washed them back into the sea. As the family disappeared up the dunes and into the car park, I scooped a handful of sloppy wet sand, and then another layered handful of dry. I fashioned this mixture into a ball, which I rolled and smoothed within the palms of my hands. Would I always be triggered? Always return to ... to what? To that June when Emma was home again, recovering in a way, but also still photosensitive and immune-compromised, in maintenance treatment, when all of the doctors' early rules continued to apply?

How can I explain? When you're in it, it is so out of the ordinary that it becomes the only ordinary you know. It becomes what you always see. A teenager on the bus with a shaved head, the parents packing up at the beach because 'you know your sister can't stay all day', the boy whose face is pressed against the night-time glass and the dad who comes by just to deliver an overnight bag—all of these things, they become something else.

Or at least, they ought to.

It really was early that morning when I went to work. It was early, and then it was late. It was a tiny pinprick mark on one of Zoe's calves, no bigger than the stamp of a ballpoint pen.

Everything happened so quickly after that.

Simon calling for a vomit bowl.

The sirens like fire alarms. The lights on the call-screen flashing for Zoe's room. Catherine shivering as though a lifeguard had lifted her from the sea. And beyond all of this, Zoe lay in and out of what looked like a half-sleep. There was blood, and it was black, and we all knew— *I knew*—that black came from the gut, from a lesion or an infection. The lights flashed on: every single light in the room. All the brightest lights. We switched them on. The doctors were flashing their lights into Zoe's pupils. The linoleum seemed to slope beneath my feet. Catherine drew her arms around herself. Then she made a noise—like a curlew in the depths of the night. As every doctor and every nurse found their place around the room, Catherine dropped her arms to her sides and surged forward. The doctors were checking Zoe, checking her all over, and Catherine surged in the same way as a wild animal surges when her cub is in danger.

It looked like a bruise: exactly the same as all the other bruises on her legs. The leukaemia kids: they came in full of bruises. Zoe had at least fifteen or so, all of them dark and purplish black. From a distance, they seemed the same to us, but Catherine saw one for what it was: odd, different, unlike the others, not actually a bruise, but the infection the doctors were searching for.

It took ICU just seconds to come.

I grabbed Catherine's hand. I brought her forward. I took her right up near Zoe's pillow. It shocked me, her hand, how rocklike and icy it had become.

We used to dig for water, Emma and me. After she returned from hospital, we used to visit this same beach much more than we visited the lake. We used to swim all year round. In the summer, footprints seemed to zigzag from the top of the dunes all the way into the water, but in the winter, it was runners' lines that we found. In the winter, the water was choppier and more purple than we ever thought possible, and the shore was awash with shells, seaweed and driftwood. We were lake kids, deep in our hearts. That's what we were. We were of the lake and from the lake, but those June months onwards, our mother shifted our play more solidly towards the ocean.

It was winter, and the sun was always low in the sky. Winter, and we visited the beach either early morning or late in the afternoon. That very first time, though, Emma and I did not hold back. We tucked our dresses into our knickers, splashing and kicking until our hemlines soaked. There was life to us, a life we had forgotten to have. I splashed Emma, and Emma giggled and kicked a splash back. We played in the sand, both of us, even Emma, who glanced at Mum and then waited until she received a quick, approving nod in return. Mum explained that the beach sand was fine, that this sand did not pose the same dangers of bacteria as the sand surrounding the lake or in the playgrounds, but neither of us truly cared for the details. What we wanted, really, was the freedom we once had. Emma and I built castles and dug seep-wells. Emma pressed her arms deep into the tunnels and flooding moats, and I sat by her side making boondies in the same way people on the opposite side of the world might have made snowballs. I layered sloppy wet sand with powdery dry and smoothed down a growing ball as if I was shaping mortar.

We took those boondies, Emma and I, and we threw them, exploded them right into the sea.

THE BOY AT THE LAKE

23

It was June when my mother and Emma returned from the hospital, June when we created the routine of our winter beach and June when the cracks finally snapped my parents in two. Mum drilled Dad's good kayak into brackets on the carport wall. She weeded the garden and mowed the lawn. All that Dad had neglected to do since Emma went away, Mum cleaned again. She changed the grotty sponges, swept cigarette butts out of the shed and scrubbed mould from the bathroom shower screens. She washed the windows and wiped smudges off the walls. Dad was there in the house and there on the couch, but he was no longer a figure that moved alongside the rest of us. Then, just as he finally found himself a job flying in and flying out to drive a truck up north, Mum packed him a suitcase, sat him down and quietly asked him to leave. Dad said he knew he hadn't been a good husband or a good father. He had his stuff too. He was sorry, he said. But Mum stood firm. 'It's not healthy for Emma. It's not healthy for any of us. I want you to go wherever you were before Emma and I went away.'

'Is this what it's all about?' Dad asked. 'I'm sorry,' he said again.

Mum shook her head. She said something or another, and then so did Dad, and it was all okay, the same kind of tennis match argument that Harriet and Samuel might have had, but then one thing led to another and Dad's voice rose. It rose and moved and ended with, 'But you're partly to blame.'

Mum stopped for a moment. 'I think you should leave,' she said. Then she stood, as if standing up was Dad's cue to go.

That was when Dad broke Emma's Barbie boat. He picked it up and paused. He picked it up, paused and then he banged it so hard against the kitchen tabletop that shards of pink plastic cut across the room.

Mum stayed cold. 'You can come back at the end of your roster to collect the rest of your things. Including *your* broken boat. Which I don't want in the carport anymore.'

That afternoon Dad accidentally put his car into drive instead of reverse, and as he smashed the front bonnet into the brick wall of our carport, both the neat suitcase my mother had packed and a large sports bag stuffed with last minute clothes and the shape of shoes flew forward. 'Shit!' Dad said, 'Shit!'

When Dad next returned, he rang our doorbell and then he stood with his legs astride and arms crossed, not facing my mother as she opened the door, but facing the actual street. He didn't turn to look at her. He didn't look at any of us. Emma rushed forward, but I held back. I watched from the hallway as Emma wrapped herself across his legs. He picked her up, twirled her around, put her down, but then discarded her there. Mum went right out to meet him. There was a coldness to her that seemed to say if she could help it, none of what we went through would ever repeat. Dad turned his back once more. All I could see was the largeness of it, the roundness in his shoulders and the broadness of his stance. I thought of his fist in that cupboard door, the strawberries and the outline of his boot in the dirt. I thought also of my mother: how quiet she had become, and how practical and inward we all were.

The first thing that happened was that Dad took Emma and me out for the day. He had come by and he had asked for us, and then before we knew it, he was back behind the wheel of his smashed-up car, tooting the horn while Mum made our lunches, wiped Emma full of sunscreen and reminded us to grab our hats. We buckled in, both of us in the back, Emma clutching Yellow Bear, and me with a clear lunchbox of salad vegetables on my lap. As Dad started the ignition, our mother pointed towards this box through my open window. 'Look after your sister okay, drink plenty of water and eat what I've given you to eat.'

Dad switched the radio station on, turned the volume high and reversed out onto the road. Football talkback smothered whatever was left of my mother's voice. A minute passed, and another. Emma reached out to lie on my lap, and I shifted to the middle seat where I held her in an awkward, seatbelted hug. I traced my finger around her ear. I placed my hand protectively along her cheek. We drove for ages, it seemed, but then we had only gone around the block. At Harriet's place, someone hammered a 'FOR SALE' sign down into the front lawn. Harriet was there, and the person hammering was there, and the pictures on the signage were all the rooms I had once take refuge in. As we passed by, I leaned forward and then turned to see it all once more through the rear-view window. I wasn't imagining it; Harriet was selling her house.

'Go back,' I wanted to say, 'Dad, stop. Turn around,' but then I didn't quite voice my words, and so instead of making a circle to where I really wanted to be, we ended up at the park, Dad intent on teaching us football. Dad kicked the ball and we tried our best to mark it. Dad showed us how to drop punt and how to torpedo. We learned to kick facing the laces of the ball away from us and towards the places and people we were aiming for. We had fun, the three of us. For that brief moment in time, I didn't think of Harriet or Emma or me having to look after her. I didn't remember the way Dad was when Emma was sick. Instead I thought, it would be okay in the end, having Dad fly-in-fly-out and not having Mum and Dad together.

For lunch that day, Dad took us for ice-cream at the petrol station down the road. A little bell rang as we walked through the door. The strips of coloured plastic at the entrance sounded like thunder. Dad slid the freezer door open. Condensation stuck to the glass. 'What are you having?' he asked.

'A Drumstick,' I said.

'And you, Emma?'

Emma grabbed the largest, pinkest packet of salt-and-vinegar potato chips, the lunches our mother had packed wilting in the back seat of the car.

The second thing that happened was that I became scared. In my room, late at night—after Dad dropped us home, after Mum said, 'What did Emma eat?', after she shook her head in that disapproving and exasperated way, after she put Emma to bed and woke her again for a midnight syringe filled with the kind of 'keep out of reach of children'

medicine that required gloves to prepare, after lights out, after it all—
Emma coughed. In the middle of the night, when everything else was
still and quiet, Emma coughed. She coughed again, and something
happened to my stomach. I thought about Dad, and us, and the salad
vegetables we didn't eat. I thought about Mum scrubbing the house,
Samuel dying, and the FOR SALE sign that had suddenly appeared
outside of Harriet's house.

Emma coughed, and I remembered the chips she ate, the salt in them,
and the lake-salt too, and Harriet and Samuel, and how one salt was
better to my mind than the other. I remembered the way Harriet had
argued with Samuel over food, and how food was important to my
mother too. I thought of my mother's face after Dad brought us home,
the lunchbox untouched, and I wondered what caused Emma's sickness
in the first place, and what it was, and how could we make sure it never
happened again? Then, for a long while, all I could think of was that
packet of chips. It was large and shiny and pink. It was red-light food.
That's what we would have called it back in primary school.

It was quiet, dark and cool. I had an extra blanket, but my toes were
still cold. There were funny shadows in the hallway, funny shadows
outside the window, funny shadows on the ceiling. I did not feel thirteen
anymore; I felt nine or eight or seven all over again. The sheets twisted
around my body. I touched the wooden headboard. Wood always made
me feel safe, but this time I couldn't stop the thoughts inside of me.
A beam cracked up past our ceiling. Harriet came to mind, and then
Samuel. I thought of my mother. Mum always said people didn't just die
and go to heaven. She told me that in her religion—in ours—people died
and then for forty days, they floated through all their haunts. They said
goodbye. They made sure their loved ones were okay.

The third thing that happened was the 'UNDER OFFER' sticker that
suddenly appeared in a diagonal across the glossy metal pictures of
Harriet's kitchen and lounge.

At the very next market event, Harriet sold her artworks in a flurry that
felt more like a post-Christmas sale than a stall in a rural town. Harriet
rung up her till and rung it up, and in the meantime, I stood there, a rock
amongst a surging crowd. Someone purchased the blanket that used to
hang on Harriet's wall, and someone else the new quilt Harriet had only

recently made. Out went Harriet's clay sculpture of a book and also her flowerpots. Out went her soaps, a series of bottles filled with salt, a set of dishes. Far in the distance, someone put the canvas painting Harriet had made of Samuel into their car boot. Samuel's clothes, his books, his binoculars were all marked, '*Free* to good home.'

'Harriet!' I shouted.

Harriet placed her hand along my arm. 'Grace,' she said, taking a pause to think about how she might respond to my distress. 'Sometimes it's better to share a story. Don't look back remember?'

'No!' I wanted to say. 'No!' because my mother was the sort to separate what was unwanted from what to treasure, to clean her cupboards at the first hint of stress, to look forward, but she was also the type to understand that there were artefacts—tapestries, handwoven rugs and memories—that she would always keep.

I took Samuel's binoculars then, and also the solitary teacup that Harriet often liked to drink out of. I took them and stood at the counter, and Harriet nodded and wrapped them for me, as if I too were just another customer.

'Harriet,' I said. She was my centre, my certainty when I was scared. 'Harriet,' I repeated. 'What if you go, and then ...'

'Shhh,' she comforted. 'Take one of these too.' She handed me a bottle of her distilled salt and added, 'You always have the lake.'

The fourth thing that happened was the sudden rain that came when my mother told me that she and Emma had to go to hospital. It was dark all at once, and cold, and what I heard was, 'It's okay Grace,' and 'Don't be silly, it's okay,' because somewhere along the line, I had realised that Emma still had to front up for monthly chemotherapy and blood tests and lumbar punctures. 'You knew this,' Mum said. 'You read her protocol.'

It was June. Dad was driving his truck at his job up north and Harriet was packing to leave our town. Perhaps I was on school holidays. Perhaps I didn't want to stay behind. Maybe it was because my mother sensed I ought to go with them, but somehow, Mum let me tag along to Emma's appointment.

At the hospital, I sat on the edge of Emma's bed and watched as she coloured in pages of rainbows and mythical animals. Familiar cries still came from the treatment room—they came and came—but they were someone else's now, not my sister's, and they contrasted sharply with the quick and quiet, 'Ouch-ouch-ouch,' that Emma let slip when the nurses needled her skin.

Emma barely lifted her head from her drawings. Whereas before it was me that confirmed her name and matched her wristband to her medicines, this time it was Emma who said, 'I am Emma ... and my patient number is ...' In her scratchy pre-primary scrawl, she wrote this same patient number around the edges of her colouring pages. She wrote her patient number over and over again and bordered pictures of unicorns and ponies in.

Not a while later, I overheard my mother tell another mother that she and Dad had separated and that soon they would sell the house. Then Mum said that given everything, the city made more sense.

'What?' I said.

Mum replied, 'Honey, it will be for the best.'

That afternoon, the nurses taught me what the numbers on the blood pressure machine meant, what to press when the intravenous line was done dripping its liquid into Emma's veins, and the careful steps to take when it came to deneedling my sister and all her friends.

I disinfected Emma's wound as one of the nurses drew a needle back. She said, 'You're a natural, Grace. Bet my bottom dollar you end up one of us.' She placed a small, circular dressing over Emma's port.

She warned both Emma and me, 'Don't forget: no swimming, pools, sandpits. No anything. Not until that wound scabs over and heals.'

At home, Emma taped a large button beneath Yellow Bear's armpit. She said, 'Shall I count one, two, three or just do it?' and when Bear replied in her whispery voice, 'quick, quick, quick, do it,' Emma stabbed the button hard with a sharp lead pencil. She patted Bear and wiped Bear's tears. She said, 'Oh what a good girl you are.'

Bear wore a bracelet of paper around her wrist. It was coloured red and scribbled with an inky marker. 'Bear's allergic,' Emma told me. She puffed her cheeks out and pouted her lips to show me. 'That's why she wears a red hospital band instead of a white one.'

'Is that what happened to you?' I asked, and Emma nodded so slowly that I felt the gap of our experiences grow between us.

The day moved towards night. The rain was heavy and constant.

The phone rang—Dad and Mum all over again, arguing, or not

arguing. My mother held the receiver away from her ear.

Emma started crying.

I cuddled her. I said, 'What's wrong?' and when she didn't reply, I asked, 'What is it?'

She said, 'There's a shadow in the window.'

I looked out of the window. There was nothing. In the kind of voice that I thought my mother might use, I said, 'It must be your imagination.' And then I said, 'Come Emma, let me make you a glass of Milo.'

I had the milk warm in the cup and the Milo mostly dissolved when Mum finally rested the phone against her ear again. She covered the mouthpiece with her hand. 'Emma, Grace,' she said as if we were one and the same. 'Do you girls want to talk to Dad?'

Both of us shook our heads.

'I'm sorry, no,' our mother apologised into the phone, and then, after a few more minutes, she added a swifter, 'Okay then. Bye.'

'Grace,' she checked, as she walked out of the room, 'are you right with the milk there?'

I nodded. When I finished, Emma took the cup from me, but then just as she started to leave, a large undissolved brown dot of chocolate appeared at the top. 'Emma stop,' I said.

But she didn't stop.

'Emma, stop!' I repeated. I tried to take the cup, but she started crying all over again. 'Hang on,' I said, showing her a spoon. 'I just want to fix the dot.'

Emma tugged the cup one way, and I tugged the other. She started up again. 'Oh no!' she was crying. 'Oh no!' And then she was wet all down her pants and on her legs.

There was a noise in my head, a buzzing. I stared at Emma, and then at the floor. For a small moment, I thought we had spilt the milk, but then the tiles were wet and clear around her ankles.

'Mum! Emma had an accident!'

The landline rang again. 'Can you answer that, Grace?' my mother called from somewhere deep within the house.

'Mum!' I shouted.

The phone rang out, but it didn't matter anymore. I needed to fix this. I needed to look after Emma. I took Emma to the bathroom and ran a tub of water. While I left her there to get undressed, I went back and mopped the puddle up with a wad of toilet paper. The paper went yellow, and then the sogginess smeared all over the floor. I remembered the germs: we were not allowed to have germs. I took the dishwashing detergent and poured it all over the yellow mess, and then I poured a bowlful of water too. The floor went bubbly and foamy.

'What happened?' my mother said, coming into the room. 'Oh Grace, what did you do?' she said, gently taking the detergent from my hand.

Emma was in the bathtub, naked and already sitting upright in shallow bubbly water. I washed her with a soft cloth. I washed her port too. As the dressing slipped off in the water, it struck me just how protruded and awfully foreign this port was.

The last thing that happened was Emma. In that bath, vulnerable and covered in a more contained version of white and soapy foam, she turned to me and spoke both with the depth of her eyes and with the childlike sound of her voice. 'It's not a treat,' she said.

'What's not?' I replied, confused.

So, she broke the syllables up for me. 'The TREAT-ment room,' she said, passing bubbles from palm to palm.

24

When I was thirteen I took my sister to the lake. It was June, I was thirteen—going on fourteen—and suddenly it came into my head that I needed to take my sister to the very place that was out of bounds not only with Dad but also now with Mum. I had it in my mind that if we went to the lake, if I took my sister, if she breathed the air in the same way Samuel had taught me to breathe, if she heard the bubbling that I had heard, then everything would be alright. I packed food for the two of us, grabbed water bottles, hats, sunscreen and even Harriet's special salts. Emma carried her yellow bear just as she once did at the hospital, and without us letting anyone know the truth of what we were doing or where we were going, we began to edge towards the boundaries of our backyard—first on the trampoline, then on a picnic blanket that we lay beneath the shade of a tree, and finally, after our mother had come out— dishtowel in hand—to check on us, and after she had smiled approval at our play and returned back into the house, we lifted ourselves over the fence, and took off down the road. Emma was all giggles and laughter. I remember repeating my mother's words: 'Emma we're going on an adventure.' I echoed them in the same way Emma's voice once echoed on the concrete underpass walls.

Emma told me that one of the nurses once took her on an adventure, that she had been in her room for so long and that her nurse had decided to do something to cheer her up. 'Come with me,' she had whispered and they ran down hallways and in and out of stairwells and that at the end of it all, the nurse unlocked a secret door that opened to the back section of the fairy garden where no-one happened to go. The nurse gave Emma an ice-cream in that part of the garden, and our mother and the nurse chatted while Emma played in what she said was the magical dolls' house. She said it was a good adventure. She asked what ours was going to be.

'The lake,' I said. 'Like all of those times before. Emma, you'll see. I'll show you. You'll see and breathe things different to the way we used to.'

It was sunny that day, completely opposite to what winter was supposed to look like. We were wearing shorts and t-shirts, and our hats and sunscreen were both safely on. At the clearing, just before the landscape opened towards the bushland that led to the lake, Emma beamed as though she was unwrapping a present or waiting while Mum lit candles on a birthday cake, and then there it was: our lake deep with water, the thrombolites completely immersed and golden in the sun. We dropped our backpacks and ran down along the jetty. At the viewing edge, Emma held onto the railings and leaned right over as if trying to soak as much of the lake in as possible.

'Emma!' I shouted.

She pulled back, looked at me and smiled.

We stomped on the jetty, made noises, danced, ran from one side of the railings to the other. It was so nice to see her run. Her hair was short, her skin still pale, but she was running and her gait was almost like it used to be. If I squinted my eyes a little, I could imagine everything returning to almost to normal again.

I went back to our bags, pulled out Harriet's jar of salts, held it close to my face like a wish, and put it back. 'Emma, pause,' I said, wanting to silence all our noise. 'Can you hear that?'

Emma stilled her movement. She stood completely frozen in action, like a bird waiting for the most subtle ripple on the water's surface. She shook her head. 'What is it?'

'Listen for the bubbling,' I said.

Emma closed her eyes, visibly straining to hear what I could hear.

I told her all that Samuel had told me: that the lake was as old as time and the thrombolites made the air we breathed. I said, 'Can you feel how much cooler it is here than back where we were walking?'

She nodded. 'It sounds like bubbles.'

'Yes,' I said. 'Open your eyes now. Look into the lake. Can you see the pale blue strings?'

It was like giving her a world within the world. She leaned over the railings once more, looking for the strings. She squealed when she finally found them. I said, just as Samuel had said, 'Breathe those strings in, Emma.'

She took a huge gulp of air. We both did.

'Can we play now?' Emma asked.

We picked up our backpacks, retreated from the jetty and made our way to the walking trails where we then diverted off-path so that we could go down towards the banks. Before I knew it, Emma was digging in the sand, making a seep well just as we had made at the beach. She was scratching the earth for the water table and for the upswell that always came in such a rush.

'It's my favourite thing,' she said to me.

Vaguely, I remembered the nurses' warnings. For a moment, I thought about the soil at the lake being different to the sand of the ocean. I heard my mother's voice: patchy details reminding us that the two were not the same. Deep in my memory were the rules: no pools, no sandpits, no crowds. But all of this was softened by the rules of my own living. I had stirred the dots, counted the right steps, carried the salts, taken Emma to the lake, let her breathe the way I had. I had soaped the floor, touched the wood, whispered, 'Goodnight, sweet dreams, see you soon,' and added the word, 'alive' in my head.

I knew that the treatment room was not a treat, that Yellow Bear endured pencil stabs of needle pain, and that our mother intended to pack up our home just as Harriet had. I wanted Emma with me— there at the lake—where I thought we belonged. I wanted to play just like we used to, before. So, I lathered her in sunscreen a second time and reminded her to keep wearing her hat. I fed her cucumber, dried apricots, crackers—all the things she liked—and I let her play.

We built sandcastles, made boondies and dug that well so deep that we cut through layers of soil, each darker than the layer before. Our skin, our faces and bodies all became sweaty and itchy from the unseasonal heat, but we kept digging until finally water rushed up in cold and murky swirls. Emma pooled that water in the cusps of her hands. Then she splashed it all up into the air. When it fell, it landed in fat drops. Fat drops on our bare arms. On our clothes. On the ground. We laughed like we had not laughed for so long. There were things I noticed but also didn't quite notice. The dirt beneath Emma's fingernails, for example. The way she lifted her shirt to scratch an itch along her torso. The redness already spreading outwards from her recently needled port site.

She said, 'Grace, I'm hot.' She scratched her itch once more. She moved away from the well and came to sit on my lap.

'Take a drink,' I said, reaching into her bag for her water bottle.

She drank that water in gulps. 'I'm hot,' she repeated.

Her body was so much hotter than mine, but her hands were still cool from our water play. I stood her up, grabbed our drinks, the salts and Yellow Bear. The rest of our belongings, I left behind.

'Come Emma,' I said, handing her the bear.

She was my shadow once more, my twin, nine years apart, always following me, always by my side. But then she began to lag. I turned back and took her hand, not yet registering that Yellow Bear had already fallen from her grasp. It was clammy, her hand, warmer than before, but I held it tight and led her down to the boardwalk and onto the jetty. I took her to the railings where we had played only that small while before. I said, 'Listen.'

'I'm hot,' she told me once more.

Desperate now, I said, 'Take a deep breath, Emma. It will cool you down.'

On the jetty, I held my little sister's hand, and then quite suddenly I wasn't holding it anymore. I remember no people, and then people everywhere, the coolness of my palm and the reassuring, resurgent warmth of someone else—a boy now—holding my hand again. In a moment, Emma was gone, and then not gone. I can describe in vivid detail the feeling of that new warmth: a roughness, me, that other hand, the way we stood shoulder to shoulder, the edge of the jetty, the water below, the thrombolites. I had wanted their oxygen, their miracle. I had wanted the cure we had all overlooked. I can describe these things, but the ten or fifteen minutes beforehand, those minutes are as patchy as my mother's warnings. They are uneven shapes in my memory, excavated holes that sometimes flood like water through those seeps.

I was thirteen. It was June. Emma slipped out of my grasp. I didn't notice it at first. It was the slightest letting go of me. But then the sound that came was this: thud. Hard on the jetty planks. I remember calling her name. 'Emma!' Calling it. 'Emma!' I remember kneeling by her side. Shouting, 'Help! Somebody help!' Shouting it so many times. Emma in and out of consciousness, like that. There and not there. And then there again, long enough to throw up. I was kneeling next to her, looking at the convulsions of her body over her arm and the tar-like substance that came from within her. I could hear the buzzing that must have been in her ears. I could hear bubbles. Emma was clearly too sick for walking, but also too sick for staying. I wriggled beneath the railings and out over the jetty. I scooped up handfuls of water, which I splashed straight onto Emma. I was trying to heal her, trying to listen, trying to be like Samuel and Harriet. She had slipped right out of my grasp. She had fallen hard onto the jetty planks. She fell just as Yellow Bear had fallen. I had the salts in my bag. I had Harriet's voice: 'You always have the lake.'

We had snuck down. We had played, wanting to play in the bushland and the banks in the same old way we used to. We had breathed the air. Listened for bubbles. Felt the coolness. It wasn't a long time. It can't have been. If I think about it, then maybe it was long enough for Mum to finish the breakfast dishes, make the beds, tidy up, have a shower and put a load of laundry on. She wouldn't have checked on us again until she came out to hang wet clothes on the line. A couple of hours maybe? That free space between breakfast and lunch? But then things happened so quickly, and all of a sudden, Emma was too sick to even cry for home, and I was scared because I didn't know whether to run for help, or to remain by her side. She was in trouble and I was the boss, the eldest one, and that meant 'if anything should happen to Emma, I'm holding you responsible.'

'Help!' I called. I shouted it as loud as I could. 'Help!!!' The salts and the lake: they simply were not working.

Then just as I felt I had no other choice but to leave her and to head at least to the winery restaurant, a woman came along, and then a group of people, and a boy. All of them sprinting towards us. The next thing I knew, somebody was by Emma's side and somebody else—the boy from the hospital, the brother, Nate—was holding my hand. While all the adults took over, Nate held my hand. We stood side by side, looking at my sister and the commotion and the lake.

'What happened?' one of the adults asked me. She had tapered nails and red varnish. The colour of the varnish was so dark it reminded me of Mum's painted Easter eggs.

I answered whatever fragments I answered.

In the background someone else said, 'I've called an ambulance.'

Nate was holding my hand, and then holding me. He held my hand. He was not with David, nor his mother or father. He was there with the woman who had the red manicure. I didn't yet know who she was. An aunty maybe? A big cousin? She looked like she was caring for him. David was not there. And neither was their mother. Nate held my hand. I didn't want to let go. We spoke through our fingers. There was touch and there was warmth and there was a pressure which found a voice.

Then the woman with the manicure handed me buttered bread sprinkled with sugar. She looked after me just as Harriet might have. She had tapered nails and red varnish. I stood at the edge of that lake, Nate and I holding each other and eating that soft white bread, the sugar shining like salt, the butter thick and warm. The sky was blue, the nails were dark, the bread was white and soft. I tried to eat, but the food didn't seem to fit down my throat. There were people, lots more people than I had thought. There was a helicopter too, and sirens. Those sirens, they made so much noise.

Then the place swarmed with ambulance officers, and my mother was there, and Harriet carrying Yellow Bear along with her. Mum kept pushing forward but the paramedics kept holding her back. She said, 'I don't know what to do. I don't know what to do,' but she knew just fine, because in all that commotion, she broke through barriers and found her way to Emma, where she sat patting Emma's hairline and reciting stories in the same soothing voice she might have used if she were reading a book. 'Once upon a time,' she said, 'there lived a mother. Now this mother had big responsibilities: she took care of crops and the land, but she also took care of her little girl.' Mum told the story of Demeter stronger than I ever remembered. This mother. This child. No-one would break their bond. The hospital bag was already packed. It was always already packed. It had a stuffy odour, all bleach and toothpaste and soap. You have to smell it to know it; it never leaves you.

◦ ◦ ◦

At the hospital, I painted the lake. Somebody handed me acrylics, and I painted the sunshine, and close-ups, and all sorts of pretty things. My canvases were pink on the edges, purple in the centre, and at the top there were lots of shiny bright dots—a hundred and eight to be exact. I don't know why I chose this number or the repetition, just that I did. Time seemed to stop. I sat in waiting rooms, in hallways, on the other side of ICU. My mother couldn't tell that these were paintings of the lake. The close-up confused her. She said how pretty the canvases were, how imaginative, how calming. She asked what the word was to match my feelings.

I don't recall answering. What I recall instead was the sense of waiting, like there was nothing else to do but wait. I recall being cold and helpless, and my mother coming in and out of those heavy ICU doors. I recall being behind Emma as she was finally wheeled back down to her normal ward, and then later—days later—her hair, how rejuvenated it was, how utterly out of place it seemed amongst all those tubes and monitors. I recall holding onto to Harriet's bottle of salts. And then, of course, I recall the photographs. In my mother's wallet, there were pictures of my sister as baby, pictures of both my mother and Emma sitting in the passenger seat of the car, and pictures of the cradle of my mother's arms. I felt it then: this great, aching absence because there were no pictures of me. All I could see was how pretty my mother was, how perfectly arched her eyebrows were, how clear her skin, how symmetrical her face. Emma looked like her. Everyone at the hospital said so. I was the smart one, the artistic one, but Emma was beautiful, *breathtakingly* so. 'Oh, what a beautiful child,' the nurses said. 'Look at your eyelashes, coming along like that.'

'I'm not the smart one,' I used to think. 'The smart one would never have put Emma in danger the way I did.'

There were other things too. Like the way my mother diverted her gaze when I asked after David. Or like David's mother—quite alone—walking into one of the consultant's offices and closing the door.

25

And then, back home, we all dressed in our most colourful clothes even though when Samuel died we had all worn black. We went to a church we didn't normally attend. It was far away, and we drove for a long time slowly past a lot of paddocks and trees, and when we arrived, as cheerful as we had been told to be, the inside of the church was dark, and everyone was crying. I told myself not to cry. The coffin was a lot larger than what I thought it would be. I suppose when people lie down they appear bigger somehow. It was white and glossy, that coffin. There were flowers across the top, but also toys: an old teddy, a water gun and a videogame controller. Everyone was looking at it all as if they were looking at television. They kept saying 'Rest in peace.' They were kissing the coffin and saying, 'Rest in peace,' and I wondered why no-one said 'rest in peace' to those of us who were still alive and who therefore needed the reminder to rest more. I said it in my head, to my mother, to me, to the people who were not in this room, and especially to Nate and his mother, who stood so silent and so still. Then someone else said something about God, and God's way, and the mysterious workings of God, and I caught myself in a yawn, not because I was bored or tired, but because everything was heavy and smoky with incense, and I needed more air than I had.

The priest cleared his throat. He was wearing a big embroidered gown, and when he stood at the front of the congregation, he spoke about innocence, goodness, the importance of being grateful for what we have, and the fear of losing what we consider can't be lost. He said something about all of life's work too—all of it being suffering and love and preparation. Everyone grabbed their tissues and dabbed at their eyes. He kept talking about 'preparation'. Hard things were preparation for the next lot of hard things and for the lot after, everything growing and hurting more and more, until finally we had what it took to help ourselves and others attain an afterlife. This was what it was all for—this time and all the horrible times we had beforehand—just preparation to help other people, and preparation for life and death.

● ● ●

At the cemetery, sand kept getting into my shoes. The grains were scraping near my heel and in between my toes. I couldn't help but think that under a magnifier, the sand would be like shells on a beach or smoothed-over glass.

There were a lot of birds. There were a lot of people too. Nate was near, and when I looked at him, I remembered the way Emma often fell asleep next to me, and the way the space between us, a space of sisters, felt like the only place where we belonged. Then I thought of the lake-stench on her clothes, her sweaty skin, and also of that hard port, and the way it always looked like something aliens had implanted, and I remembered the sight of it in the bath, and then the ambulance and the paramedics. How they ripped her clothes off and lay her down. How they stretched her arm up and knew straight away to examine that port. How I stood back as the inflammation grew out of that bump like a bruise that darkened and swelled. How my mother could not hold back. And how the nurse's warning returned to me: no swimming, no sandpits, no germs until the wound had healed.

And then, somebody handed out these bright balloons. We all counted, 'One, two, three ...' and let go. The sky was dotted with rainbows and colour, but one balloon lagged below the rest. I stood there, looking up for such a long time, because looking up was less confronting than seeing everyone, absolutely everyone, touching and hugging and touching Nate, without David, like that. I watched those balloons. Like bath bubbles lost to the sky.

Afterwards, we returned to the car again and drove until we were back at our house, and then somehow while we were gone little sandwiches had appeared, and soft drinks, and cake. Nate came too. He sat next to me at the breakfast bar and started peeling the label off a lemonade bottle. I liked having him near. I liked those moments when his leg brushed against mine. We didn't speak about the lake. We didn't speak at all. We didn't need to. There was something unspoken about him. He kept peeling at that label, at the sticky stuff.

The sandwiches were coming around, and people were talking, but there was no particular conversation, only a hum. Nate kept peeling, and the label fell in tiny shreds on the laminate. In the background, Emma stayed close to our mother's legs. She held a freshly washed Yellow Bear tight in her arms and she did not let go. In the meantime, Mum lit a candlewick in a small brass bowl filled with oil. She did that, my mum. It was how she prayed. In the kitchen window, the flame flickered and reflected and seemed double what it was.

Nate ripped the lemonade label. So many people knew him. They spoke to him. They touched him. Someone gave him a card and a gift, and he sat there mouthing the words that were written inside. For the shortest second, I was sure he said my name. He said, 'grace' and 'God's grace', and his whispers were warm, but they were also sad. Then the sandwiches came around again. It was as though they were floating, those sandwiches. I shook my head. No, I didn't want any. Yes, I was okay. Yes, I knew I ought to eat, something, anything, but no, not these sandwiches—they were too heavy, too bready, too chickeny.

It was Milo I wanted. That's what it was. It calmed me in a way, spooning that Milo into my cup and filling it with milk. It was the action of something to do. That was what was so appealing. I put my cup in the microwave. Nate kept ripping at the label. It was quiet between us. Then I looked at him, and he looked at me, and I gestured towards the milk. It was body language, completely silent, but he knew enough of what I was trying to say, because he shook his head at about the same time as the microwave beeped. My Milo had crusted over the top of the milk. I cut through that thick film of chocolate with a spoon, and I thought, 'You better get rid of all those dots, or else.' Or else what? Or else more of the worst things would happen.

I heard my mother's voice before I saw her face. She said, 'Are you two okay?'

I jumped, and as I did so, I accidentally hit the cup with my hand and it fell onto its side. The Milo spilled onto the bench, dots and all dripping down onto the cupboards. Brown milk poured like speckled paint onto a white board.

Nate went outside a long time before I did.

It was sprinkling. Somewhere along the way the weather had turned. It does that sometimes. It happens like that. You wake up and it's blue and bright, but by afternoon the clouds have gathered, and the shade has spread across town. Or else it starts the other way: clouds over a wet road that dries as the day goes by.

No-one noticed when I grabbed an umbrella, and no-one saw me walk to the bottom of the driveway. The road out the front of our house was worn out. There were grooves in it, small valleys where the tyres most often went. I walked along those grooves and made my way to the lake. It was *my* lake. No matter what had happened. It was the place I chose whenever I wanted to be hidden and shielded from view. Normally, you couldn't see much beyond those trees unless you walked right in. That's all it took for Emma and me to hide the way we did.

Maybe that was why they were chopping the whole front line of trees down. There were workmen, a cherry picker, chainsaws and branches crashing to the ground. The men were dressed in orange vests. A woodchipper was parked on the verge. There was so much noise. They were chopping the last tree—the tree I used to sit against back when I was struggling to read.

Nate stood beneath that wet grey sky. I went to him. I held my umbrella above both our heads. He said, 'It makes me sad.' I think those were the first proper words he really said that day: 'It makes me sad.'

I said, 'It might be because they were sick anyway. Sometimes that happens. These trees: they sometimes die from the inside.'

He said, 'Not just the trees.'

It was four thirty. The branches were crashing down, I was still wearing the clothes I had worn to church, and Nate was too. Then the cherry picker backed away and the men came down. The tree looked odd, half-lopped and skinny, branches high in the sky like that.

Nate said, 'They're killing it, you know. They're not giving it a chance.'

I said, 'They might just be trimming it a bit,' even though I knew from the other stumps this was not true.

I had goosebumps and I was hungry. The workmen began to chainsaw the tree at its base. They cut from one side, and then the other. It took three of them to push it down, two to chop it into logs, and one to throw it all into the woodchipper, churning like that.

We counted seventy-three rings, and then Nate said, 'It was a tuart.'

There were birds in that rain and then the birds were elsewhere. Nate rested his hand on the stump. He said, 'Touch it.'

It felt tender, surprisingly damp. I asked, 'Who was that lady, the one you were with that day? You know, here?'

He said, 'Sherilyn? She's our neighbour. She brought me here for lunch.'

That was all he needed to say. I could see it in his face then. His brother and mother. His dad too. All of them in the city, at the hospital, last days, and him left behind. They say you suffer twice. You suffer in the first instance, and then again in the memory of it all. I wondered, even then, what he must have remembered when he happened upon Emma and me at the lake? And I wondered also, what I was remembering when I called to my mind the warmth of his hand.

A workman came up to us. I thought he might tell us we had to go, but all he said was: 'Have you seen my thermos?'

I asked, 'Were the trees sick?'

The workman said, 'These ones were visual obstructions. We had to get rid of them. You know, after the two girls and all.'

Nate picked up a pebble. He flung it hard through the air, but in the end, it hit nothing, just bounced on the dirt and rolled to a stop. He said, 'It's not the tree's fault.'

The thermos guy replied, 'Hey mate, I just did what they told me to do.'

Lightning started, and the thunder too, and the workmen went home. Nate and I counted the seconds between one lightning bolt and the other, and then we waited for a proper downpour, but it stayed exactly like that, cool and drizzly. He smelled like sea salt to me, and I said so, and he replied that he had surfed in the morning, or at least tried to. His dad took him. That's what they did, before all this. They went out together and caught the winter whitewash.

I said, 'I'm sorry about your brother,' but then because he didn't want to talk about it, I changed the subject to something softer again. 'You like surfing?'

He said, 'I think so.'

That was his smell. That was how I would remember him: encased in the ocean and heady with woodchips.

We picked up leaves together. We poked at insects with a couple of sticks. 'What else do you like?'

'Guitar,' he said, miming an imaginary guitar the way some people do. Then he hummed in that voice of his.

I said, 'I wish I knew how to play.'

He put the pretend guitar in my hands and he said, 'This is E and F and G. They are first string notes.' Then he placed my fingers along what he called a fret board.

My strumming was clunky and closed (it had to be because I was a beginner). I giggled, 'I can't do this,' and so he took the pretend guitar and mimed the action of standing it against the stump.

He was in front of me. I had my hand dangling by my side, but I wanted him to hold it so much. I could feel it without actually feeling it. I thought, it's silly, me wanting to touch him like this. It's one-dimensional. It's me. Not him. It's me. It's wrong. He's sad. It's wrong.

Still, that was when we first kissed.

It was wet, clumsy and rushed. My chin chafed pink from the inexperienced mix of saliva and soft teenage stubble. I was young, I think, for a first kiss. I was mimicking the grown-ups. That's what it was. I was no different to that kindergarten kid who slips her mother's clippity-cloppity shoes on and stands in front of the dressing mirror, head at the bottom corner of the reflection, painting circles of lipstick from her chin to her nose.

We were on the side of the road near a weeping stump. We were damp with sweat and sharp drops of rain, visible where we once would have been invisible.

'Were you scared?' he asked, because I guess he was thinking about me and my sister.

'No,' I lied.

RETURN

26

'He's married,' was what I told the lady behind the counter at Harriet's old market stall when I finally returned to Lake Clifton. I stood across from her, holding a jar of olives in one hand and a ten dollar note in the other, and while she tended to my purchase, I said, 'I used to come here a lot. The lady that lived here gave me my first job.'

The woman said, 'That must have been so long ago. I bought this place years gone now,' and with even just this interaction, something unlocked within me. We talked about things back then and things since, and then after a small while, and for whatever reason, the woman asked whether I had a partner, a family.

'Not really,' I said. But then I clarified, 'He's married. He's married, and he already has a whole family of his own.' It was the first time I had told anyone.

'Oh,' she replied, without a strip of judgment in her voice.

There was more that I wanted to say, but I didn't know how.

It was warm, early afternoon. The stream of customers was as steady and as relaxed as it had been when Harriet was in charge. People walked about in loose dresses, or else in t-shirts and denim shorts. They picked things up. They put them down. Every now and then, they came to make a purchase. In the meantime, I found a painting I liked, and I said so, and then the woman behind the counter told me that it was something her sister had made. I picked up a scented candle and turned it in my hand. The wax smelled of passionfruit. I said, 'What about this?' I asked. 'Did you make this?'

'No,' the woman said. 'That one is from wholesalers.'

Another customer came to the table. That customer handed over a small clay figurine, and the woman took it and placed it on tissue paper, and as she wrapped it, she asked how this customer's day had been and where it was that she had come from. After a while, the two of them began to chat just as we had, and in that chat, I heard a distinct Greek word. I heard it, and then another, and then the women switched languages entirely into Greek. As much as I wanted to say, 'Hey, I understand too,' there was something to their fluency that gave me pause. It wasn't the recognition of words I knew or the confusion of the those that weren't familiar to me, but rather, what stood out were words I must have learned somehow, must have heard before, but never thought to use myself. I had forgotten that *arithmó* could mean 'phone number', and I liked the way the customer said *palaiatiká*, a word I took to mean 'old things' or 'ageing things' or something 'old-fashioned' but couldn't fully comprehend without a dictionary or my mum to explain dialects. I was not a confident speaker. There was fluency to my ear, a swiftness with which I absorbed the words the women said, but that fluency did not extend as far as my tongue. I thought in English first, and then in translation, and so, I stood there, unannounced, unwilling to join in because joining in would halt the very speed and smoothness that seemed to be settling me.

I placed the candle back onto the table, and as I listened to the two women, I remembered how good my mum and Emma both were at switching codes and languages. At the hospital, there were times when words and translations simply did not come, when words were thrust upon us or when words were not enough. Mum and Emma were travellers. They were always going back and forth, always moving from one way of speaking to another.

Even after Emma had her port removed, after she walked barefoot on grass and played in sandpits again, after she started school and after life slipped into what people termed our 'new new-normal', the conversations my mother had with the other mothers from the ward were always different to the conversations she had with the mothers she met at Emma's school.

At school, Emma wore two neat plaits and her uniform buttoned to the top just the same as everyone else, but at the hospital, she always seemed to walk in with her posture tall and her hair set free and long. It would strike me, how naturally this switch came for her, how innately she understood that on that ward 'hair' and 'height' were synonyms for 'hope'.

I was different though. I struggled to travel in the same way my sister and mother did. Instead I overlayed health with hospital just as I had once overlayed my Greek. In my teens, I lost count of the number of oil candles my mother burned, the children she prayed for, and the cancers that slotted easily into my widening scientific vocabulary. Before Emma, words like neuroblastoma, rhabdomyosarcoma, osteosarcoma and ependymoma could have just as easily been botanical drawings as they were religious liturgies, but afterwards, those same words felt so normal that I forgot the softer, more innocent language that I had known before.

And then, of course, there were other words too, words like relapse, recurrence and prognosis. When Emma was well again, it comforted me to be mathematical. I thought in percentages and statistics. I distinguished between her lymphoblastic leukaemia and the myeloid sort, distinguished between acute and chronic, distinguished also between David and Emma. David was older, a boy, and without a bone marrow match. Emma was the right age, the right gender and had me as her safety-net tissue-twin.

The women slipped back into English. Their Greek diminished just as another customer came to the counter. It had been a long day. 'Excuse me,' I said, now that there was nothing to interrupt. 'Is there a bathroom I can use?'

The woman behind the counter pointed towards the back of the house. She said, 'Through the reception door. There's a sign: down the hall and to your left.'

I followed the market displays around to the back. Other stalls had long since filled the place where Harriet's outdoor laundry once stood. Wooden decking had replaced the old painted concrete. Its pinkness was not local, and yet it still felt as if it belonged more than what was there before. The ground beyond that decking was pebbly and loose. Aside from Harriet's once young olive groves, the fig tree I used to hang off, and a sectioned off fruit and vegetable patch, all the other plants were dense low-to-the-ground natives. I could see why the back entrance was a now a reception. Down the side of the property, there was a small gravel parking lot.

It was strange being inside Harriet's old house again, strange stepping on the same floor I had once stepped on, strange running my fingers against the walls. The house felt as warm and as inviting as it was when I was a child, but although the layout was still the same, it seemed smaller than I remembered. The painting of Samuel had long since gone, and in its place was a fine and detailed print of a girl playing in the woods. Behind her, abrupt brushstrokes formed a blurry image of a water-deprived bush. The colours, like those of my summers, were brown, olive and orange. It was endless, this scene, and the child, in her summery white dress with a bow at the back, seemed grossly out of place. Nevertheless, it was still a print and not a painting, and it seemed chosen not for its artwork but because the crispness of the dress that matched the décor in the house. Everything around me felt at once fashionable but also generic, indicative perhaps that this was now a bed and breakfast, and not a home.

In the bathroom, though, there was a sign that made me smile. If I were to talk about my childhood, I'd hardly think to mention the calcium in our water system, but now that I saw the chalkiness on the tiles above the basin, and the neat, reassuring typeface saying that this chalkiness was harmless, I remembered how present the calcium actually was.

I washed my hands a lot longer than I needed to. I cupped them beneath the running tap and washed my face too. The calcium had lined even the porcelain of the basin. I brushed my fingertips along the fine white deposits. If I could have, I would have absorbed this calcium into my skin. I patted my face dry with a paper towel.

On the corner of the bathroom cabinetry, between the basin and the towel dispenser, was a neat display of bottles and soaps. One of the bottles was filled with salt. I pulled the cork out and shook a few crystals onto my hand. They smelt like the lake-salt. They looked like the lake-salt. They stuck to the leftover dampness on my hands like the lake-salt, but the granules were smooth, uniform and not made in the finicky way that Harriet once made. I corked the bottle again and turned it upside down. Sure enough, a production number was stuck on the base. I placed the bottle carefully back, and instead reached into my handbag just to touch the jar of salt that I had brought with me. I had forgotten how peaceful it was to even hold the bottle.

Nothing *happened* between Emma and me. We never had a falling out, nor did we drift apart. Yet, in a way, everything happened. Before her illness, Emma slept in either her own bed or mine. She always faced me, a small space between us shaped like a love heart, but once we moved to the city, she slept instead with the curve of her back pressed against Mum's stomach, or her body burrowed in Mum's arms. In the meantime, I placed Harriet's teacup, the salt and Samuel's binoculars on my dressing table like little mementos or touchstones. In my desk drawer, beneath all my study notes, I kept my tin of colouring pencils and a twelve-pack of graphites in shades *H* all the way to *9B*, and whenever a homework problem stumped me or an assignment task felt too difficult, I gave myself over to a small sketchbook.

My new drawings were not like those I had once made with Harriet. While Emma was in hospital, I had a playfulness and sense of a colour, but after Emma was well again, that playfulness gave way to detail-for-detail, monochromatic sketching. In treatment, all I wanted was to imagine, but later—as I made my way through high school, and then as I finished it—this same imagination frightened me so much that I sketched only ordinary shapes: sunglasses atop a pile of books, nail-polish bottles, mugs emptied of milk and dirty spoons left on idle plates. In Emma's sickness, colour gave me hope, but in her better health, it was detail that kept me company. Mum lit candle after candle, and I learnt how to spell a whole new cancer. Sometimes Emma came home with an odd bruise or another sore knee, and while Mum looked her over in that 'just checking you' way of hers, I retreated to my bedroom where I allowed textbooks and copy-for-copy sketches to ground my otherwise anxious brain. Then, without considering the possibility that there could be an alternative, I enrolled in a nursing degree. Nursing, like the replicative drawing I had been doing, was exact and meticulous; it focused me.

Emma, however, was different. The minute she turned eighteen, she packed her bags and boarded a plane. 'You only love once,' she said, and when I corrected her, she shook her head and replied, 'No, that's exactly what I meant to say.'

Outside again, the crowds had nearly gone. Although a few people milled about, the lady I had purchased the olives from had begun packing away her unsold stock. I had already made the decision not to stay overnight, and yet it seemed wrong to leave without a goodbye. The woman was folding tables for stacking, and it didn't seem like much of a stretch to reach out and help. I began to carry each table back to the garage, but then as I lifted the last, I felt more of the same cramping across my stomach as I had felt throughout the day.

'Are you okay?' the woman said.

'Yes,' I said, and also, 'no,' because it wasn't just an ache, it was worry too.

For a long time, I thought that those who knew cancer spoke a language that those who didn't know it could never comprehend, but really the language we all learned in hospital was as nuanced as dialects across opposite sides of a river crossing. Emma and I were speakers of similar but *different* languages. We understood each other in much the same way as those who say bonjour also understand buongiorno, or those who speak Spanish can also pick up Portuguese. Emma left in search for something new, while I chose to stay. While she holidayed and travelled, I sketched as thoroughly as I worked. At the hospital, it was mathematics that comforted me. I held onto my statistics. Like my Milo, mathematics kept me safe. So long as there was a chance, a probability—with Emma, with Tom, with Ava, with Zoe—then everything would be okay.

What I wanted was to make meaning out of a horrid thing. But horrid things are sometimes devoid of meaning. I could never seem to peel those layers back, could never access what I was before cancer, before my sister fell ill, before my nascent language was absorbed, could never understand what it was that Emma went through. In the same way as my mother sometimes slotted Greek words into the structures of her sentences, we slotted our untranslatable experiences into the rhythms of our lives. I could not know Emma, or know my mother, could not know my patients, could not know Nate, or fully even know myself. My sister having cancer, or Nate losing his brother, both of those things were always going to be like hearing the rises and falls of a language you recognise but have no vocabulary for.

27

In the car, I typed the words '*signs you're having a miscarriage*,' into the search engine of my phone. At the top of the list were all the symptoms I expected to find, but then, lower down, there was a caveat: '*Half of threatened miscarriages end in pregnancy loss. In the other half, the symptoms stop, and the pregnancy goes on normally.*' I must have read that caveat maybe six or seven times. I stared at my phone, first at the webpage and the statistics, and then later at the photograph of the sandcastle family. I scrolled through all my social media accounts in that distracted scrolling kind of way, came back to the castle family and back also to my missed and recent calls list.

'Is that you, Grace?' Nate asked after just one ring, and I nodded as though my nod could travel through the phone. He said, 'How are you?' and 'I tried calling you.'

And so, I said, 'Yes, I know,' and then I told him about Zoe at work and William from across the road.

He said, 'I don't know how you do what you do.'

'It's not work I rang about.'

'Is it the bin?' he asked. 'You were angry. I get it. It's okay. I'm sorry too.'

'It's not the bin,' I replied.

'Where are you?' he asked.

'I went home.'

'Home? Do you mean the lake?'

I nodded again, perfectly aware that a nod could not translate across a phone connection.

He said something or another then, and 'What's it like now?' and 'Did you go to Preston Beach too?'

'I did,' I replied.

And then, for whatever it was that triggered his memory, Nate launched into a story about David, that time, out in the sun for Boxing Day lunch, all of them keeping an eye around their feet because their dog Judy had barked herself into a frenzy near the water tank and they had turned just in time to see the last seconds of something scaly slithering from one side of the garden to the other where the woodpile was. Nate's dad was flipping steak on the barbecue and his mum had her salad and tongs, and then when no-one was looking, David poked Nate's ankle with a stick. 'Snake! snake!' he shouted, and Nate never leapt so high in his life. Then, because the rest of them were laughing the kind of laughter that was a long time coming, Nate had to fight not to kick his brother in the shins. It was only later, after at least a decade of Easters and Christmases had passed, when his family reminisced about 'that time you jumped fair and square into the rafters, Nate', and 'remember when your brother snake-snaked you?' that he finally found the funny side.

I felt myself soften. Time paused for a minute or two, and in that pause, I remembered something Nate had told me once before. He said that he and David were in that waiting room when Emma, Mum and I first walked into the ward. They were there, and we came in, and he looked up from the computer game he was playing, and he watched us and pretended not to, and what stuck with him most was the way I kept twisting at my skirt and then the way I needed the structure of the wall behind me. He said that I had reminded him of him. I had that look only brothers and sisters have. He recognised it. That look which was his only a few years previously.

I couldn't place Nate to that day or any of the other early days, but I could place his brother. David was so full of 'it's going to be okay' and 'always wear thongs in the shower' advice. He was the boy-in-the-robe, the-boy-in-the-hall and the boy-outside-Emma's-first-trip-to-the-treatment-room. Later, when Nate explained that this was the time David had learned he had relapsed, that things had been travelling well and then not so well, and that they were all there—Nate and David and all of them—with the R-word their mother couldn't bring herself to say, it struck me just how happy David had come across, and how fixed in my memory this happiness was. I would have recognised David anywhere. He didn't need his family by his side or the context of a hospital for me to pick him out in a crowd. For Nate, though, things were different. I was aware of him as a member of his family or as a sibling, but I didn't recognise him as a figure on his own until the day Emma collapsed at the lake.

Now, on the phone, Nate said, 'Do you remember when they chopped down that tree?'

I nodded, and he reminded me that was the day they buried David.

I said, 'I know,' because every time I thought of it, I also thought of my sister and how although she had been flown to hospital, she did recover, and she did come home, but for David there would be no more home. There would be no nieces, no nephews, no Christmas get-togethers, no 'remember that time'. I thought of the day I sat on the edge of a phlebotomist's chair stretching my arm out for a clinic nurse who strapped me up, tapped my vein and remarked how easy I was to bleed, and then, of course, I also thought of the consultant who came to say that Emma and I were as close a bone-marrow match as siblings could possibly be.

Nate must have been thinking something along the same lines because he told me he was angry that afternoon. People kept telling him that David was 'better off now,' and, 'at least he's no longer in pain', and it was making him mad at them for drawing on such insensitive things, and mad at David for dying in the first place, and mad even at Emma and me, at both of us actually, which was stupid and a mean thing to say, but it was true; he was mad at us because he heard me say, 'She's my twin, nine years apart,' and all he could think of was the fact that Emma and I had one of those matches that came as freely as the plastic-covered dinner plates the hospital orderlies brought around but as uniquely as fingerprints and the rainbows held in soap-bubbles, and all he wanted, all he ever wanted—didn't anyone know—all he wanted was to be a tissue-twin too.

And then he said he was sorry.

'No,' I said. 'Don't apologise.'

'It wasn't you and Emma really.'

'It's fine,' I said, pressing the phone close to my ear. 'Truly, it's fine.'

Something outside of my car rustled then—a possum perhaps, or even a bat—and for a moment the sound reminded me of what I had actually called to say, and then also of the boot-prints I once found in the dirt outside my family home and the strawberries that had upset my mother so much, and I paused again, not wanting to talk to Nate anymore, not wanting to do to his family what happened to mine. 'I'm sorry,' I said. 'I shouldn't have rung.'

'No, wait,' he said.

But I shook my head.

Not that long ago, we slept, we woke, we kissed, we touched. We were always so wordless, so outside of speech. That's what it was, what kept us together. People say that, don't they? When they're caught having affairs. 'She understands me,' or vice versa. That's what happened with us; we knew not to ask about those untranslatable things.

'Wait,' he said.

'I have to go,' I replied, and then I added a swift, 'Bye,' before I could change my mind.

My stomach was still cramping. Even my back ached. I pushed the phone down into my bag, way out of reach.

28

Noises, once so familiar, suddenly seemed to shift around me again. I sat in that car for a lot longer than I'd like to admit, unwilling to start the ignition or make a move forward. I reached back into my bag once more for my phone but, at the last moment, instead of calling Nate, I happened to touch the jar of olives that I had purchased earlier in the day. I grabbed that jar out of my bag, twisted the lid off and began to carefully pick out singular olives so as not to spill the oil. They were good, those olives, tangy and more sophisticated than any I would have normally bought at a supermarket or deli, and it occurred to me it was their saltiness I had wanted all along. I had looked for it along the beach, had licked it off my lips, had come back to where I knew I would find it in the brined cures and lakebeds of the places I used to know, and now, there I was, finally stepping out of the car, eating those olives like chips.

One last time, I went to the lake. I stood on the jetty as if it were a picnic blanket sewn from fabric and threaded into the kind of narrative Harriet would stitch together. This plank, for example, that I now crouched down to touch, was Emma and me, all those times, before, coming just to play. That one was Emma on the banks, arms spread loose with the lift of wings in flight. Here was the safety of wooden panels on my skin. The thrombolites against a winter's moonlit sky. Spring with my mother. Stories held in the watery reflection of clouds and the sound of Harriet not yet knowing she would soon take me in. Over there, I saw the end of summer, Samuel barefoot and leaning over the jetty to breathe those blue strings in. I saw Harriet too, sewing a life spent together, knowing already what the final patch of her quilt would entail. There she was, collecting water that she would later turn to salt. Swirls in the bath. And her voice, 'You always have the lake.' Didn't she know that I was the kind of child who would hold on to those words? To make them more than what they were?

For a moment, a bird broke my circle of thought: a little mudlark that came to perch on the railings. Overhead, a flock of galahs took speed in a triangular aerial formation. I heard a crow. But then also a thud. It rose from my heart to my throat, and before long, I was there again, another me, a second body, knelt over the waiflike and semi-transparent memory of sister. Pouring water on her skin. Holding those salts like prayer. Holding them in the hospital too. *If I hold these salts. If I keep them this way. If I always have the lake.*

'Breathe,' I thought, because that was what I had since learned to do.

I don't remember seeing Harriet much more after that day. I guess it was the natural way of things, when people move to other places. And it was right, anyway, for her to go, and right that she was not here now, but she was my mother figure for a while, and after she left, I still thought of her. I used to imagine her down by a river or along a shore somewhere, turning those months spent looking after me into one of her wall quilts, making artworks out of us, another market somewhere, new friends that she made. I wondered what fabrics she would have used, how she saw the story begin and end, and what she thought as she patched the call of my face onto one of those abstract squares. There we were, for a time, me motherless and Harriet childless. And then, there we parted. She let me go, just as she let Samuel go.

From Ancient Greece, there comes a word—*agápi*—the highest form of love. It means to love with charity. Like Harriet's name and mine. It is to love well past what you want for yourself in order to choose what is best for others. It's doing the right thing, for example, even if it means having to say goodbye. When Harriet left, I projected her very essence into her salt, as if one bottle of salt could contain not just the power of the lake it had been extracted from, but also everything that I imagined was maternal itself. I held onto that salt as we wheeled Emma from ICU to her ward. I held it as she grew. Even when she left to go abroad. I still held it now, and although I knew—logically, mathematically, I knew— that the lake did not heal Emma, that medicine did, and that there was no such thing as magic salt, even as Harriet tried to tell me this herself, there I was, all these years on, keeping this bottle because it comforted me like a mother's voice in the dark.

As I finally returned this salt to the lake, I thought about the way the thrombolites had hugged me throughout my childhood, and the way they shared their breath with me. I remembered the parties my parents threw before what was obvious to me about their marriage became obvious to them. I thought of Nate and the stories of his musical scores. I remembered Harriet—that enveloping, motherly way of hers and the stories she wore on her skin—and then eventually, I thought about the languages we had all learned—the language of loss and the echoes of sickness that somehow drew us all in need. Whenever I visited the lake— even when I came with Emma—I was always a child, always wanting protection, a bit of warmth. This time around, I saw the thrombolites lit beneath the last hearth-like reflections of the setting sun, and for a moment the lake seemed amniotic to me. The winter's depths had not yet fully receded and the still-submerged quality of the thrombolites came to my mind as embryos protected in the womb. All those years, I wanted so much to touch a thrombolite. I never knew what one felt like. Was it as rock? Did it move? Did it feel warm with life or had it hardened over time? Along hidden parts of the lake, I dug for certainty. I plunged my hands in rushing seeps. I skimmed stones and when the ripples calmed, I imagined the slow-motion twist of that stone's descent, the way it unsettled the lakebed, sediment rising from forces in motion, before everything stilled again.

I always thought Lake Clifton belonged to me. Despite what happened with Emma, I still dreamt of the thrombolites as if they were my steadfast home, but now, as I shook the last of the salt out of the jar and watched the granules dissolve into the familiar depths of the lake, I wondered if my fondness was not so much about the lake belonging to me, or me to it, as it was about wanting something that I could count on to stay the same. When I picture Harriet now, I see her as a migratory bird—a sandpiper perhaps, or a red-necked stint—who took shelter by the water's shore, who rested while she waited for winter to pass. She was not my stable thing that stayed the same. She was never meant to be. But really, neither was the lake. We all did it—Mum, Harriet and me—we all dipped our fingers into this water. We wanted to touch it on our skin. We wanted to know what lay within. The thing is, though, you don't have to touch a thrombolite to leave the damage of a fingerprint behind.

I placed the coolness of my left hand over my navel. I changed my thinking. I remembered that other thing I knew; touch was the first sense to develop in the womb, and touch, done right, could also say all that needed to be said. 'Hang in there,' I whispered to the child that I hoped was no longer under stress inside of me. Time didn't seem to matter any longer. Ten minutes was really no different to ten years. The sun had set and soon the night sky would come again, more brilliant in the country than in the city. In the spring, peppermints and bottlebrushes bloomed like they always bloomed. In the autumn, leaves would crunch beneath my boots even on the footpaths and cycleways that wove my suburban life into repetitions of work and home.

'Soon,' I said, the stress and the cramping all but replaced by a small assurance that I would handle things, no matter what they were. Then, as I turned my attention back to the car park and to the drive ahead of me, I thought about the words I ought to share with Nate, and the syllables involved in uttering, 'I'm pregnant,' and in that moment, in much the same way as I knew I could always find south again using the Southern Cross and the Pointers, I also knew those were words I was not going to say.

29

It was dark by the time I arrived home. William was sitting near my doorstep, crouched on top of his football and wearing an Auskick shirt, black shorts, fluorescent boots and socks stretched to his knees. His arms were bare and prickled full of goosebumps. A backpack and small library of books were piled nearby. In front of him was an open lunchbox filled with snacks he perhaps packed himself: a banana, a handful of sultanas and a scattering of dry and loose rice bubbles.

'William,' I said, 'Where is your jumper?'

He looked at me and shrugged. 'I'm not cold.'

'What are you doing here? Are you okay?'

'I am angry,' he said.

It was so succinct, so low in volume and directly to the point that I turned to him and said, 'I am angry too.'

'Why?' he asked.

'Some things just haven't quite gone the way I wanted them to.' I paused. 'What about you? Why are you angry?'

'The same,' he said. Then he told me that he had wanted to play football, but his aunty said they had to visit his mum and sister who were in hospital.

'Oh,' I replied, kneeling on the paving beside him. 'Yes, I understand that.'

We were both quiet, him having shared with me, and me remembering what it was like to be the one left behind. A car drove past. The old man from down the road unravelled the garden hose and began to water the front verge just as he did most evenings, although this time, he seemed to be out much later than he had ever been before. Another car drove past. It was nearly summer; football season had finished months earlier. 'William. It's November.'

'That's what Aunty Cole said.'

We were quiet again—me looking at William, and William blocking the doorway and eating one Rice Bubble at a time. 'Why are your mum and sister in hospital?'

'My sister was born.'

'Oh!' I replied, 'But that's exciting, isn't it?'

William shook his head. 'That's what everyone else says too.' His voice was deadpan flat.

'You don't think so?'

He shook his head again.

'Why?'

'Because she came early.'

'She was premature?'

He said, 'I didn't want to visit today. I wanted to play football, but then Cole made me, and when we were there I asked her if she would take me to the park, and then she said, "William," and Mum said, "Don't you want to stay longer?" and I said, "No," and Cole was mean. She said, "William, footy season is over, William, it's over."' He animated his conversation, adopted different voices for the various speakers.

'So, now you've put your clothes on to make it football season?'

'And I made my second dinner after dinner.'

I nodded to his lunchbox. 'I can see that.'

He grabbed another solitary Rice Bubble. I looked at him, and then back to the Rice Bubbles. I said, 'So if I had ten goals twelve, what would my score be?'

'Seventy-two,' he replied.

'Is that right?' I asked. 'Are you sure?'

He nodded. 'Seventy-two. Give me another one.'

'You like maths, don't you?'

'And science and football.'

'Shall we go back?'

'No,' he shook his head.

Down the road, the old man drank water out of the garden hose. His wife came out. She said something or another, and then she placed her hand along his arm and took the hose from him. She turned the tap off and rolled the hose onto its bracket.

In the meantime, William stood up, and began to bang his football against the hard metal of my boundary fence. He banged it, and then he kicked it back and forth, back and forth from the fence and then down to his hands. His technique was shaky, not as good as it was the previous evening. Sometimes he caught the ball. Other times he dropped it or kicked it wide. A neighbour walked by, out late with his dog. I looked at William, all those confusing emotions swirling about. I saw him trying to control his world.

'Laces to faces,' I said.

William paused, as if trying to remember all the skills he must have learned at footy.

'When you kick, you should face the laces up but also towards what you are aiming for. Then you have more chance of knowing where the ball will go.'

'Oh yeah,' he said, this moment of recollection arriving. Then he added, 'How do you know?'

I shrugged. 'I just do.'

William bounced and kicked the footy to himself, and then he handballed it into the air. He kicked and marked and then, just as he pulled the ball back down to his chest, his aunty came calling from across the road. 'William! I've been looking for you.'

I unlocked my front door, put my bags down, and went around to open a window or two. In the kitchen, a gust of breeze flew in, and a piece of paper fell from my bench and drifted and twisted to the ground. In the same way as a coin falls to either heads or tails, this paper had landed with my doctor's handwriting and the details of the termination clinic on top. A few years ago, I would have taken this to be a sign, but this time around, I simply picked the paper up and turned it the other way. All my aches had long since subsided. The paper was on the bench now, with the list of obstetricians face up. I grabbed a tablespoon from the drawer and placed it like a paperweight on top.

'William!' Cole sounded. 'We have to go. I'd like to take this dinner to your mum.'

Back outside, William had slumped his shoulders and pulled his ball into his hold.

'I don't want to,' William said.

'Don't you want to see your sister again?' Cole asked.

'No,' William said.

'William,' she replied, with a much smaller tone. 'I want to. Your mum wants me to. Please.'

I had been in the doorway, watching, but now I came out. 'I can look after him, if you want.'

Cole nodded and William smiled.

'Come on then,' I said, turning to him. 'It's too late to go to the park, but I'll kick with you here if you want.'

William visibly lifted. I kicked the ball to him. He handballed his footy up in the air and then back down into his arms.

'Eight goals, two?' I asked.

'Fifty.'

'Two goals, four?'

'That's sixteen,' he said and he thumped the ball right into my arms.

30

I was straight out of university when I started working on our ward, but for all I had experienced, I was still terribly naïve, brand new and without the faintest idea what to expect. On my very first day, the nurse coordinator took me around to all the inpatient rooms. I studied observation charts just as I had on my practicums and in learning hospitals before, I gave out medications and did all the usual things, but then in one of those rooms, we came across a mother who was a little worse for wear, and then before I knew it, the nurse coordinator had offered me up to, 'Hold Bub please while Mum ducks to the bathroom to brush her teeth and have a shower.' I still remember the sound of that baby's crying, the incessant, demanding sound of it, which didn't stop even after his mother returned, and I remember also the guilt on that mother's face, as if brushing one's teeth and washing one's hair were luxuries she ought to have forgone.

Next door and across the hallway, male and female voices carried the combined panic of not being able to get their sick infants and toddlers to eat, sleep or take their medicines, and then, there she was, the mother of this child, hair wrapped in a bath towel, rocking her baby, and crying, just the same as the child had, just the same as what might have been happening in maternity wards across the state. The mum held this child and did all the things that less stressed parents might have done. She changed him, fed him, and placed him softly near her heart. As they both calmed, and the mum finally had the chance to loosen the towel-turban out of her hair, I remembered all those mornings Samuel, Harriet and I had spent over the thrombolites. I remembered the sound of the lake's bubbling breath and the life the thrombolites layered and grew in millimetres over thousands of years, and I brought this sound back to the hospital and back to the gaze that the mother and son now shared.

I said, 'Are you going okay?'

'I am,' the mother whispered.

That's what it was like, that very first day.

I wrapped the tiniest blood pressure cuff around the baby's arm, and the machine made its familiar beeping noise. It was the same now on our ward as it was in the hospitals I had learned in, and as it was all those years ago, the same beep-bipbipbipbip-beeepbipbip-beep. As the cuff puffed up and the child drifted into much needed sleep, the mum turned to me and said, 'So you're new here?'

And then, not that long later, she asked, 'What made you become a nurse?'

◉ ◉ ◉

It was early on Monday when I went to work, but this time, instead of heading straight to our ward, I took the stairs three floors up to Intensive Care.

Zoe was in the isolation room, electrodes all over her chest and intravenous lines everywhere. An ECG kept stock of her heart. A pulse oximeter measured her oxygen levels. Her respiratory rate, blood pressure and CVP were sharp spikes and flats on the computer screen. She was asleep, bloated from antibiotics and naked but for a large child-sized nappy and a sheet that she had mostly but not fully kicked back. There was no getting up for her, no going to the toilet, no freedom. Her nurse worked at a desk in the corner of the room. A gentle breakfast tray of cereal and milk waited at the end of her bed.

Catherine sat in a chair close to Zoe. She was dressed for the day and up and ready, but at the same time she was unnervingly still. She wasn't reading, wasn't writing in her journal, wasn't flicking through magazines. Instead, she breathed in and then out, matching the rhythm of her breath with the rhythm of Zoe's breath. Only when the nurse moved to take a vial of blood from Zoe's IV tube did Catherine finally notice me. She said, 'Every four hours they test her sugar and take her blood, and then because she has so little of it, they IV it all back into her system.'

I said, 'Yes. That's right. They can do that.' And then I said, 'I wanted to see that you were both okay.'

'We are,' she replied. 'In a way. But yes, they're happy with her.'

'That's good to hear.'

Catherine looked through the glass partition into the part of ICU that allowed high-demand but not critical patients to be roomed together. She nodded towards a young boy not more than six or seven years old, and also towards the life-sized teddy at the base of his bed. 'What's he going to do with that bear?' she asked. Then, without waiting for a reply, she added, 'I'm sure they meant well.'

'Have you family here?' I asked. 'Support?'

Zoe shifted in her sleep. As best she could, she rolled a little to the side.

Catherine said, 'I'm tired.' And then, 'Her brother is with his grandmother. She and I spoke a few minutes ago. She says they were playing pick-up sticks and dominos all weekend, but at the same time, she also says he's missing Zoe.'

Outside, a motorbike revved its engine. It was so loud and sharp that Zoe's body tightened. She looked like a baby lying half-naked in a nappy like that. I almost expected her arms to fly open and her hands to jerk into little spread-out stars. Behind the motorbike, a police siren whirred in that speeding ticket kind of way. As far as sirens went, it was nothing at all, but even so, it still brought to mind pictures of my sister, long ago, suddenly septic along that jetty. In my heart, it always felt like the difference between life and death that day was in the way my mother recited stories for Emma, and also in the way she touched Emma's face while Emma slipped in and out of dizzying consciousness. Everyone else was loud and panicky over Emma's cold limbs and dropping blood pressure, and there was my mother, amongst paramedics, helicopters and me—a frozen, frightened me—touching, gently touching, keeping Emma there, keeping her wanting to be alive.

On Friday, Catherine had done exactly the same: as ICU came, and as doctors swabbed Zoe and talked quickly about sepsis and bacteria, Catherine had suddenly calmed herself at the top of Zoe's bed. In the kind of voice that mothers use when they're sending their healthy children off to bed, she said, 'Zoe, I'm going to read you a story ... here I am Zoe, I'm right here ... Zoe, listen ... *Ever since he was a puppy, Yappy yapped. He yapped after breakfast. He yapped at lunch* ... Zoe, look at me. Can you show me your beautiful eyes? Look at me.' Zoe looked, and as she did so, Catherine patted her hairline and her forehead. She read on, '*He yapped until the sun set and the moon came up.*'

I turned now towards Zoe's sleeping face. ICU was several floors above ground and our windows were thick. It made me question whether or not I had actually even heard a motorbike and a set of sirens or if those things had come from inside of me. Nevertheless, at least for a time, those sirens seemed to have stopped. I said, 'Zoe is a beautiful name. Do you know that it's Greek for 'life'?'

'I do,' Catherine said.

And then I said, 'It's hard for the siblings too. About her brother, I mean.'

Maybe there was something in my voice or my manner that Catherine picked up on, because she looked at me in this soft way and said, 'What's your story?'

'Pardon?' I asked.

'What's your story,' she repeated. 'Why did you become a nurse?'

Rarely did I ever reveal my past to patients, but this time, it felt like the only thing to do. I said, 'My little sister was also sick. Way back. When we were both just kids. Same as Zoe. Same cancer.'

Catherine shifted the way she looked at me. I don't know how to explain it, just that it was as though we were no longer nurse and mother, but rather two people with somewhat parallel lives.

I kept going. 'A little way through her treatment, she also had sepsis. Bacteria had infected her via her port. She had the same as Zoe, the same leukaemia.'

'Is she okay now?'

'Yes,' I said. 'She's well. Though she really is very much the "you only live once" type. She's in Europe, backpacking.'

Catherine lit up as much as a woman whose child was in ICU could possibly light up.

I stood there, not sure what to say or expect next. It wasn't as though my long-ago pain suddenly had a purpose or a reason, nor that I thought

Emma's story could somehow comfort or connect with Zoe's mother. What it was, was this: I understood now what we had been through. I was only just recognising it. Mum, Emma and I hadn't ever much talked about it. We were a 'don't look back' family, at least on the surface. We kept pushing, carving our lives forward. Time was a line, a never-ending string that stretched from before and moved well into after. But Emma had been in ICU too. When we were little, we dug a seep, Emma and me. Sometimes time burst like water. Sometimes a straight line tangled into a knotty sling.

I looked at Catherine and then at Zoe. Just as Zoe's doctor came in to check on her, Zoe roused out of sleep.

'Hey, sweetheart,' Catherine said. 'You're awake?'

Zoe scrunched her face into a small pout. Her room here was both full and also bare. Everyone seemed to come forward—her nurse, her doctor, her mum—but at the same time, there was nothing warm about ICU. It was stark and metallic with the shape of everything clinical. Catherine edged herself even more closely towards Zoe.

Zoe's doctor washed his hands and then he read the nurse's observation notes. 'Hi Zoe,' he said. 'How are you, today?'

Zoe looked towards all the tubes and wires that were stretching from her to the block of monitors behind her. 'I'm hungry,' she said.

'Great!' the doctor exclaimed. Then he pointed towards Zoe's legs, which were partially covered with the bedsheet. 'Can I look at your dressing?'

Zoe nodded, and both the doctor and the nurse washed their hands a second time. The nurse pulled back on the sheet and also on the dressing. Then the doctor examined the wound and the sutures beneath. Everything looked clean, not yet healing, but also not as frightening as before. As soon as the doctor finished, the nurse took a quick disinfecting wipe at Zoe's wound. She patted it down and then covered it once more.

Just before the doctor left, he gave Catherine a reassuring nod. 'If she keeps on like this, a day or two, most of these drugs will be gone.'

Catherine busied herself with Zoe's breakfast. She poured milk onto plain Weet-Bix and then she passed the tray and bowl over to Zoe, who sat up now and ate quickly and independently. In the meantime, Catherine turned to me and said in voice much too low for Zoe to hear,

'On Friday, the surgeon who cut the lesion out said it was likely hospital borne … she didn't have the immunity … this normally harmless thing … it was eating at her leg … is this what happens, is this what I have to expect?'

'No,' I said. 'It's rare. You're unlikely to experience it again.'

Zoe finished her breakfast and pushed her bowl away. 'Butter toast?' she asked.

I looked at my watch; there was ample time before my shift began. 'I'll organise it,' I said to Catherine, and then I asked if she'd like a coffee.

Catherine nodded. Just as I turned to leave, she fit one last thought to the list she had echoed before. She turned to Zoe and said, 'Bet you'll also be the backpacker type.' It was there, in the structures of her speech. I heard it and understood it. 'Bet you'll also be the backpacker type.'

I thought of those words out in the hall, and then again as the elevator rattled back down to our ward. How we did it too. Me, Nate, everyone. Always trying so hard to bring our futures into time.

It was early when I walked through our doors, but already the smells of the breakfast rounds wafted through the corridors. In the family room, I pressed thick fresh slices of wholemeal bread down into the toaster. I placed a couple of small packets of wrapped butter onto a white plate. I frothed milk in the coffee machine—a latte for Catherine and a plain babycino for Zoe.

Acknowledgements

I wrote *Skimming Stones* on Whadjuk, Pindjarup and Wardandi Noongar boodja, and I wish to pay my respects to Noongar Elders, past, present and future for the ongoing care of the places I always draw so much inspiration from.

This novel was originally submitted as part of a PhD, and for that I thank the University of Western Australia for providing me with support, scholarship, mentors, peers, community and a space to learn. I especially wish to thank Brenda Walker for her committed and empathic supervision, her fine eye and unwavering belief in me.

Thank you also to my previous teachers, particularly Julienne van Loon and Ann McGuire, who played such an integral role in the early development of my writing.

In 2020, *Skimming Stones* won the City of Fremantle Hungerford Award for an unpublished manuscript. My gratitude to the City of Fremantle and Fremantle Press for supporting new novelists like me through such an award. Thank you to everyone at Fremantle Press including Jane Fraser, Claire Miller and Georgia Richter. Georgia, I am especially grateful that you understood the heart of my project and I feel lucky to have you as my publisher and editor.

Special thanks to Maureen Gibbons, Bindy Pritchard and Dee Pfaff for our nurturing writers' group and for always inspiring me. Similarly, thank you to my sisters, Nicole and Pam, for our interesting and intelligent conversations, many of which spark ideas that wind their way into my work.

Inspiration comes from all sorts of places and I would like to thank Annamaria Weldon for her research at Yalgorup National Park. This research put me in mind of a childhood memory, sent me exploring and later prompted some of the first passages that went on to frame this work.

I would also like to thank a woman I have never met but whose writing reached me at a time I needed it to. In 1955, Sonja Goldstein kept a diary of her son David's treatment in an early paediatric oncology ward. I am deeply grateful that Sonja kept such an account and that she shared it willingly through time and space in the hope that it might 'be of help to others'. It was. Thank you.

Deep emotional appreciation to everyone at Perth Children's Hospital and to organisations such as Telethon Kids Institute, Children's Leukaemia & Cancer Research Foundation, Kids Cancer Support Group, Kyle Andrews Foundation, Ronald McDonald House Charities, Perth Children's Hospital Foundation and many others. To the researchers, consultants, doctors, nurses, medical and support teams within these organisations, all of whom work tirelessly to care for cancer families through difficult times, thank you.

My biggest thanks are reserved for four people. To Mum and Dad: I love how you have always supported and encouraged me. Amongst many other things, you taught me to dream, and you taught me to work—two qualities useful in a writer. And finally, to my beautiful children: I am truly blessed to have you in my world. Thank you simply for being you.

Also available from Fremantle Press

Richard runs his alternative healing centre from an old houseboat in a scrapyard on Trusting Lane. The *Little Mother Earth Ship* provides spiritual sustenance at regular meetings of the Circle of IEWA. While Richard plies his new-age wisdom, disciples Finn and August help to run the centre. But warning letters from the council are piling up down the side of the fridge and the arrival of a new mystic, Celestiaa Davinaa, is about to rock their world. How many alternative healers can one small boat hold before the enterprise capsizes?

'Mel Hall has created a thoughtful story about the quest for personal meaning, exploring themes of invisible illness, sexuality, community, faith and spirituality.' *Books+Publishing*

online at www.fremantlepress.com.au

Also available from Fremantle Press

On the cusp of summer, 1986, Rowan Brockman's mother asks if he can come home to Septimus in the Western Australian Wheatbelt to help with the harvest. Rowan's brother Albert, the natural heir to the farm, has died, and Rowan's dad's health is failing. Although he longs to, there is no way that Rowan can refuse his mother's request as she prepares the farm for sale. This is the story of the final harvest—the story of a young man in a place he doesn't want to be, being given one last chance to make peace before the past, and those he has loved, disappear.

'Few novels have such quiet authority and insight into pasts and futures, nostalgia and grief.' *Toni Jordan*

and at all good bookstores

First published 2021 by
FREMANTLE PRESS

Fremantle Press Inc. trading as Fremantle Press
25 Quarry Street, Fremantle WA 6160
(PO Box 158, North Fremantle WA 6159)
www.fremantlepress.com.au

Cover image from istockphoto.com
Cover design: Nada Backovic, nadabackovic.com
Printed by McPherson's Printing Group, Victoria, Australia

 A catalogue record for this
book is available from the
National Library of Australia

ISBN 9781760990640 (paperback)
ISBN 9781760990657 (ebook)

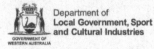 Department of
Local Government, Sport
and Cultural Industries

Fremantle Press is supported by the State Government through the
Department of Local Government, Sport and Cultural Industries.

Publication of this title was assisted by the Commonwealth Government
through the Australia Council, its arts funding and advisory body.